BABYSITTERS' HAUNTED HOUSE

We looked up at the widow's walk. I imagined Mary Randolph standing there in her white dress . . . every night . . . for twenty years. Even in the midday sun I shivered. I wondered if Mary was now spending her nights haunting the mansion? Or was someone else—Georgio, perhaps—trying to make us *think* the Randolph mansion was haunted?

Also available in the Babysitters Club Mysteries series:

No 1: Stacey and the Missing Ring
No 2: Beware, Dawn!
No 3: Mallory and the Ghost Cat
No 4: Kristy and the Missing Child
No 5: Mary Anne and the Secret in the Attic
No 6: The Mystery at Claudia's House
No 7: Dawn and the Disappearing Dogs
No 8: Jessi and the Jewel Thieves
No 9: Kristy and the Haunted Mansion
No 10: Stacey and the Mystery Money
No 11: Claudia and the Mystery at the Museum
No 12: Dawn and the Surfer Ghost
No 13: Mary Anne and the Library Mystery
No 14: Stacey and the Mystery at the Mall
No 15: Kristy and the Vampires
No 16: Claudia and the Clue in the Photograph
No 17: Dawn and the Halloween Mystery
No 18: Stacey and the Mystery of the Empty House
No 19: Kristy and the Missing Fortune
No 20: Mary Anne and the Zoo Mystery

Look out for:

No 21: Claudia and the Recipe for Danger
No 22: Stacey and the Haunted Masquerade
No 23: Abby and the Secret Society

BABYSITTERS' HAUNTED HOUSE

Ann M. Martin

The author gratefully acknowledges
Jeanne Betancourt
for her help in preparing this manuscript.

Scholastic Children's Books,
Commonwealth House, 1–19 New Oxford Street,
London WC1A 1NU, UK
a division of Scholastic Ltd
London ~ New York ~ Toronto ~ Sydney ~ Auckland

First published in the US by Scholastic Inc., 1995
First published in the UK by Scholastic Ltd, 1996

ISBN 0 590 13737 9

Typeset by Contour Typesetters, Southall, London
Printed by Cox & Wyman Ltd, Reading, Berks.

10 9 8 7 6 5 4 3 2 1

Summer vacation has just started, and I allready have a two week baby-sitting job. I'm taking care of Karen and Andrew Brewer. Karen is seven years old and Andrew is for. Evry day, for two weeks, I'll be finding ways to entertin them — and hopefuly myself. I hadn't expected to start my summer vacatin whith a full time job!

Claudia

That was the first thing I wrote for my summer English project. I had to write a l-o-n-g essay during the holidays. That's because I didn't exactly pass English this year. (You may have noticed that my spelling's pretty bad.) I'm one of those people who have a lot of trouble with writing and reading. Even when I try my best, I'm always making mistakes in spelling, and I'm a very slow reader. Don't feel too sorry for me, though, because I'm talented in anything that has to do with colour and design. (Sorry if that sounds conceited, but that's what everyone says about me.) My friends say I've got a unique sense of style, too, and it shows in the way I dress. I've got this knack for putting odd pieces of clothing and accessories together in ways that really work. I just haven't got a knack for putting letters and words together.

Luckily, my English teacher, Mrs Hall, understands my problem. She gave me extra help during the school year. But I still failed. Mrs Hall was almost as disappointed as I was. So she came up with this idea that if I wrote a very good essay over the summer, maybe I could raise my grade in English to a passing level. When I asked her what I should write about, she said to write about anything I wanted and that it could be fiction (you know, made up) or non-fiction (something that really happened).

I like fiction, especially mysteries. I'm a big

Nancy Drew fan. But as I'm not the type who can imagine stories like that and write them down, I was left with nothing to write about but the truth. So I decided to take notes on what happened to me every day, like a diary. Towards the end of summer I'd read through my diary and use it as an outline for an essay. The day I wrote my first entry in my diary was the day I agreed to sit for Karen and Andrew Brewer.

I got the job through this great club I belong to—the Babysitters Club, or BSC. In fact, Karen and Andrew are the stepsister and stepbrother of the BSC's chairman, Kristy Thomas. Kristy is chairman partly because she started the club, but mostly because she's the best person for the job. She's bright and well organized. She also has a take-charge, no-nonsense kind of personality. Believe me, that's what you need to keep the BSC running smoothly.

Anyway, as I said, I began the notes for my summer writing project with that entry about babysitting for Karen and Andrew. As I closed my notebook I was more than a little worried that my essay was going to turn out to be boring with a capital "B". Why would Mrs Hall—or anyone else for that matter—want to read about me and a couple of kids looking for things to do on hot summer days? It would end up being a boring story about people trying not to be bored.

As it turned out, what happened to me, my

friends, and our babysitting charges was as exciting as any made-up story, even a Nancy Drew mystery. I could never have imagined that soon we would all be spending two weeks in a *haunted house.*

1st CHAPTER

Claudia

The last week of school before summer vacation went on fourever. And it was hot! The temprature was over ninty evry day. When the school year was finely over, my freinds and I were jumping out of our sweaty skins with exsitment. We had all sorts of ideas about how to celabrate. Whitch is what we were talking about at our first Baby-sitters Club meeting of the summer.

"I say we start the holidays off with a day at the shopping mall," I told Dawn Schafer, Mary Anne Spier and Shannon Kilbourne. "I need loads of art supplies. And some beads for making earrings. Besides, the mall's air-conditioned. What do you say?"

"I'm babysitting all day tomorrow," Dawn replied. "For the Prezziosos."

"I'm sitting, too," Mary Anne said.

"Then let's have a sleepover tonight," I suggested. "One with pizzas, ice cream, the works. This is our summer holiday, after all!"

"I'm sitting tonight," Shannon said.

"Me, too." Mary Anne, our club secretary, was looking through our babysitting schedules in the record book. I'll tell you more about that in a minute. "And Claud, you're scheduled to sit for the Newtons. Actually, we're all pretty booked up this week. Especially you, Kristy."

"Good!" Dawn, Shannon and I said in unison.

We blamed Kristy for our fuller-than-ever workload during the first week of the holidays.

"Why are you lot giving me a hard time?" Kristy asked. "I told you, if we turn down jobs at the beginning of the summer we'll look bad."

"Come on, Kristy," Dawn said. "A day or two off wouldn't have ruined the club."

"Everyone needs a break," I added. "We've all been studying and taking exams. One of us even

6

has *homework* this summer." I bit into a Twix for comfort.

"I'm sure you'll do a good job on the essay, Claud," Mary Anne said. "Don't worry about it." Mary Anne cares a lot about people's feelings and tries to make everyone feel good. But even sweet Mary Anne wanted a break from sitting. "It does seem as if we're awfully busy," she told Kristy.

"Look," Kristy said, "you lot elected me chairman. I'm just carrying out my duties. I know what's best for the club."

After a few seconds of stony silence we started talking again about what we would do with our free time, if we had any.

"The beach," Dawn said. "I'd jump into the sea and not come out till the end of summer."

Out of the corner of my eye I could see Kristy watching the clock. She was determined to start the meeting on time. No slacking just because it was holidays!

I suppose it sounds as if all we do at our meetings is argue. But it wasn't five-thirty yet, so the meeting hadn't officially started. Besides, everyone was still keyed up after the last day of school. Anyway, I'd better fill you in on all this Babysitters Club stuff.

The idea of the BSC is that we work together to provide a babysitting service. We meet three afternoons a week—Monday, Wednesday and

Claudia

Friday—from five-thirty to six. Our clients know that's when to phone to make babysitting arrangements for their kids. The BSC always meets in my room. Why? Because I've got my own phone line, which means our club calls don't tie up anybody's family phone.

Another feature my room offers is a good supply of junk food. I collect it and share it. No one goes hungry during a BSC meeting, not even Dawn, who's into health food. That's why, while we were complaining about our overstuffed schedules, I was looking for something healthy for Dawn to eat. I found an unopened bag of rice cakes under my bed and handed them to her. "I got these for you," I said. "Though you could just chew on shredded paper and it would taste the same."

"Not to me," Dawn said with a grin. "Thanks, Claud."

"Don't mention it. It's my job as vice-chairman, right?" Actually, I *am* vice-chairman of the BSC. I don't have many official duties, but I take my unofficial ones—such as snack-providing—seriously!

I plopped down on the bed next to Dawn and opened a bag of cheese twists. "I still wish we'd planned a little time off," I told Dawn.

"Me, too," she replied. "Maybe I could have gone back to California for a few days." Dawn's our alternate officer, which means if one of our officers is absent she takes over her job. (Our club has eight members at the moment, by the way.) But lately she's been *alternating* between California and Stoneybrook. Dawn's father and her brother Jeff live in California, which is where Dawn lived before her parents divorced. Recently, Dawn spent a few months with her father and brother, but now she's back in Stoneybrook where she lives with her mother, her stepfather . . . and his daughter, Mary Anne Spier. The same Mary Anne Spier who's our BSC secretary.

Here's the great thing. Mary Anne and Dawn were best friends before their parents got married. Now they're sisters, too. In a way, I think that makes things even harder for Dawn. She's torn between her California family and her Stoneybrook family. She loves them both and enjoys the life in both places.

I think if it were up to Mary Anne, she'd vote for Dawn to live with her in Stoneybrook all the time. She really loves being part of a family with a mother, father and sister in one house. You see, when Mary Anne was a baby, her mother died, so for years and years it was just Mary Anne and her dad. Then came the happy ending: he re-met and fell in love with his old high school sweetheart, who also happened to be Dawn's mother! The rest is history—happy history for Mary Anne.

As I said, Mary Anne is secretary of the BSC.

Claudia

That means she keeps our record book up-to-date. The record book is not to be confused with the BSC notebook. We all write in the notebook about every single sitting job we take. Then we all read the notebook once a week. That way, we keep up on how things are with the different kids we sit for. No one gives me a hard time about my bad spelling. But writing in the notebook isn't one of my favourite things to do.

Mallory Pike (Mal), on the other hand, loves writing in the notebook. She wants to be a children's book author and illustrator one day. So, for Mallory, writing in the BSC notebook is just practice for her career as a writer. Mallory's a terrific babysitter. She had a lot of experience looking after kids before she joined the club. She's got seven younger sisters and brothers, including ten-year-old identical triplet boys. Jobs at the Pikes' always require two sitters. (By the way I've only got one sibling—my sister Janine, who's sixteen.)

Mallory is one of the two junior officers of the BSC. The other is Jessica Ramsey, known as Jessi. They're called junior officers partly because they're young (Jessi and Mallory are eleven while the rest of us BSC members are thirteen), and partly because they aren't allowed to babysit at night yet, except for their own brothers and sisters. Jessi and Mal both love sitting and are extremely responsible.

Jessi's got an eight-year-old sister, Becca, and an adorable baby brother called Squirt. Jessi's a terrific ballet dancer. She goes to classes in Stamford, which is the city closest to Stoneybrook. Jessi and Mallory are best friends.

My best friend, Stacey McGill, is a *former* member of the BSC. In fact, she's also my *former* best friend. Recently, there was a big fight between Stacey and the BSC, and as a result of that she left—or was fired, depending on who's telling the story. She and I haven't completely made up, but at least we're talking. No one else in the club is even speaking to her. It's still a big mess, and I'm pretty upset about it.

Stacey was the treasurer of the club. Dawn, as the alternate officer, has taken over that job.

With Stacey gone, Shannon's been coming to the meetings more often. Shannon and Logan Bruno (he's Mary Anne's boyfriend) are associate members of the BSC. They're both responsible sitters we can call on at a pinch.

Anyway, there we were, still trying to work out how we could fit a bit of fun into our overbooked lives, when suddenly Kristy yelled out, "This meeting of the Babysitters Club will come to order." I think it was the second time she'd said it because she sounded a bit angry.

Jessi, Mallory and Mary Anne said, "Sorry, Kristy," and gave her their full attention. But Dawn, Shannon and I kept on talking. What finally shut us up was the ringing of the telephone.

"Hello, Babysitters Club," Kristy said cheerfully into the phone. She was glaring at us. "Oh, hi, Lisa," she continued. "Yes, we're all glad that school's over . . . No, we're working just like always. No one's going on holiday for a while."

Dawn, Shannon and I groaned—quietly enough so that Lisa wouldn't hear, but loudly enough so that Kristy would. Jessi and Mallory gave us a Look. I think they were rather shocked at how unprofessional we were acting. Mary Anne looked as if she wanted to groan, but didn't. She would never do something that could hurt Kristy's feelings. Kristy is Mary Anne's other best friend. They've known each other since they were in nappies.

"Two weeks starting tomorrow?" Kristy asked Lisa. "OK. We'll get right back to you."

Kristy rang off and looked around the room at us. "Lisa and Seth need a sitter for Karen and Andrew for the next two weeks," she said. "Seth's assistant in the workshop has broken her wrist. Lisa's going to fill in for her."

I told you that Karen and Andrew are Kristy's stepsiblings. Their father, Watson Brewer, is married to Kristy's mother. I suppose this is as good a time as any to tell you about Kristy's big, extended Brewer-Thomas family. When her mother married Watson Brewer, Kristy, her mother and her three brothers—Charlie (who's seventeen now), Sam (fifteen) and David Michael (seven and a half)—moved into Watson's mansion. (Yes, Watson's rich, *very* rich.) Karen and Andrew live with their mother, Lisa, and her second husband, Seth Engle, half the time, and stay with their father and his family the other half. (They swap houses every other month.) There's one more child in this extended family—Emily Michelle Thomas Brewer. She's a sweet two-and-a-half-year-old that Watson and Kristy's mother adopted. We all love babysitting for Emily. So does Kristy's grandmother, Nannie, who looks after Emily while everybody else is working or at school. Nannie lives in the mansion, too.

Anyway, Kristy gets along really well with Andrew and Karen. Whenever a babysitting job comes up for them, Kristy has first choice.

"Mary Anne," Kristy asked, "am I free to sit for Karen and Andrew?"

"You're booked pretty solid during those two weeks," Mary Anne said. "We'd have to do a lot of swapping around."

"Who else could do it?" Kristy asked.

"If Mallory could take Claudia's job on Friday morning with the Newtons, Claud could do it," Mary Anne told us.

"Fine with me," Mal said.

"Then I'll take the job for Karen and

13

Andrew," I said. I suppose I was feeling a bit guilty about my bad attitude earlier in the meeting. Looking after Karen and Andrew would be a lot better than going to school every day. At least I was still on holiday from school.

"Great," said Mary Anne.

The phone rang again. "I'll get it," Dawn said. She picked up the phone, smiled at Kristy, and said cheerfully into the receiver, "Hello, Babysitters Club." I suppose she was feeling a bit guilty, too.

2nd CHAPTER

Kristy

I knew you guys wanted a break when school let out, but I was afraid it'd be bad for business if the BSC members turned down jobs. Then after the last meeting, I was worried that I'd destroyed the club spirit. Now, I just want to get out of Stoneybrook and have a break myself. You guys were right. We could use a change of scene. How about a seaside vacation in a quiet town?

15

"So Karen says that Andrew and I should pretend we're animals—only she'll tell us which ones."

While we were waiting for our Wednesday BSC meeting to begin, Claudia was filling us in on her job looking after my stepbrother and stepsister, Andrew and Karen. They're great kids. I wished I could have taken the job.

Claudia lifted up her mattress and rescued a bag of humbugs she'd hidden there.

"What animal did she tell you to be?" I asked.

"A pony," Claudia said. "Only I had to walk backwards on my hands and knees so my ponytail would be. . ."

Dawn and I finished the sentence: ". . . a pony's tail."

"Right," Claudia answered. "And she told Andrew he was a frog. Which of course he loved."

Claudia plopped down on her bed, tore open the bag of humbugs, and handed it around. "But here's the best part," she said. "Karen made herself a parrot. A *talking* parrot."

We laughed. It was just like Karen to make up a game that let her be the only one who could talk! I love the way her mind works.

By then Mal and Jessi had arrived and it was time to begin the meeting.

I think Dawn, Shannon and Claudia were sorry for having behaved so unprofessionally at our last meeting, because everyone quietened

16

down before I even said, "This meeting of the Babysitters Club will now come to order." To tell the truth, for one of the first times I can remember, I wasn't really in the mood for a meeting myself. I'd been playing softball with some of the kids on my softball team (the team name is the Krushers and I'm the coach). I was thinking that Claudia had a point. Maybe we did all need a holiday.

The meeting went along in the usual fashion. There were three calls in the first fifteen minutes. We shared out the jobs and called the clients back so they'd know which sitter to expect. Then Lisa Engle, Karen and Andrew's mother, called.

I answered the phone. By the time I'd rung off, everybody else was practically jumping out of their skins with curiosity. It had been a long conversation, and they'd only heard my side of it. Which meant they'd heard things such as "seaside town" and "mansion" and "I'll have to ask Claudia."

"What?" they asked in unison as I rung off.

"Here's the set-up," I said. "Friends of Lisa and Seth—people called Menders—have just inherited a mansion in Reese, Maine."

"That's an old whaling town on the Atlantic coast," Mary Anne said. "I've read about it in a travel book. I was—"

"Mary Anne!" Dawn shrieked.

"Sorry," Mary Anne said. "Go on, Kristy."

Kristy

"So," I continued, "Mr Menders inherited this mansion from an uncle. The thing is, the Menders don't know if they want to live in it."

"Why wouldn't they want to live in a mansion?" Claudia asked.

"Maybe there are ghosts in it," Dawn teased.

"They're not sure if they want to move out of Boston," I explained. "They've got two jobs, four kids and a life in the big city."

"Reese is a pretty small town," Mary Anne added. "It's one of those resort towns with only a couple of thousand people. But the population doubles or triples in the summer."

"Anyway," I continued, "the Menders are going to go there for a long summer holiday. They've invited Seth and Lisa to stay for ten days to help them decide what to do."

"Does that mean Seth and Lisa don't need me to sit?" Claudia asked.

"They're hoping that you'll go with them to look after the kids. The adults want to be free to explore the area. The Menderses have this idea that they might open a health food shop. And as Seth is a carpenter and knows a lot about building, he can help them look at possible properties and tell them how much it would cost to do them up.

"Didn't you say that the Menderses have got four children?" Claud asked. "With Karen and Andrew, that makes *six* kids I'd be looking after."

18

"Don't faint yet, Claud," I said. "Lisa thought of that, too. She'd like another sitter to go along and help with the Menders kids."

"I'll go," Dawn said. "I love the Menderses' idea of opening a health food shop. I could help them. I've been in enough of them."

Mary Anne spoke up. "I've read all about Reese and I'd love to go there. I mean if Dawn doesn't."

"I'm sorry to disappoint you," I said, "but since Karen and Andrew are my stepbrother and stepsister, it seems like I should be the one to go."

Claudia and Dawn gave me nasty looks. I suppose they were still angry with me for insisting that we work hard at the beginning of the holidays.

Shannon said, "I don't want to go anywhere for the next few weeks. I'll be away at camp for the whole of August. Count me out."

Mal and Jessi had been quiet through this whole discussion. At last Mal said, "I'd love to go. I'm used to looking after a lot of kids."

"It'd be so great to get away," Jessi said wistfully.

"Listen, you lot," I said. "I'm supposed to call Lisa right back. She needs *one* extra sitter and *five* of us want to go. What am I going to tell her?"

"Well, I don't even know if my parents will let me," Claud said.

Kristy

I realized that none of us had permission.
(Though I was pretty sure I'd get it without any
trouble, as I'm related to Karen and Andrew.)
"OK," I told the others. "I'll ring Lisa back and
tell her we're finding out who can get permission
to go. But as whoever goes leaves on Saturday,
we'd better have an answer for Lisa by our Friday
meeting."

"Let's ask Logan to come to the meeting,"
Dawn suggested.

When I arrived at Claudia's for the meeting on
Friday she greeted me with, "I can go. I've
already started packing." All over her room—our
BSC meeting room—were piles of clothes, and
Claud was dragging her huge suitcase out of the
wardrobe. Claudia never goes anywhere without
a zillion changes of clothes.

Next, Mary Anne arrived. "Wait till you hear,"
she said. "Reese is the most amazing place.
I'd love to tell the Menderses all about it.
They'll definitely want to live there." She was
carrying two library books on the history of
Maine and a travel guide to New England seaside
towns.

Just then Dawn came bounding up the stairs
and into Claudia's room. "Great news. My
mother said I can go, no problem. Actually, Mary
Anne's dad said she can go, too. And do you know
what I did? I went over to the health food shop

and asked them how they opened the shop, where they buy wholesale. . ." She held up a notebook. "I took notes for the Menderses."

"The sitting job is for the kids," I said crossly. "Not the parents."

Shannon and Logan ran into the room right behind Dawn. Then Mal and Jessi turned up. "We couldn't get permission to go to Reese," Jessi said.

"But we can take over the day jobs of whoever goes," Mal added.

"Great," I told them. "Then I can go. Between Mal and Jessi for my daytime jobs, and Shannon for the night ones, I'll be covered." I reached for the phone. "I'll phone Lisa."

Dawn clapped her hand over the phone so that I couldn't pick up the receiver. "That's not fair," she said. "Kristy, you're the one who said we all had to work. Now *you're* going on holiday."

"But Karen and Andrew are part of my family," I said. "Besides, it's not a holiday. It's a job sitting for four kids. And I've got permission."

"Well, I've got permission too," Dawn said.

"Me too," Mary Anne said.

"Me three," said Claud.

"I'm the chairman," I said. "There wouldn't be a Babysitters Club without me."

The phone rang. Dawn took her hand away so I

21

could answer it. (I was feeling pretty bad about how I was behaving—extremely bossy and more than a little selfish.)

The caller was Lisa, wanting to know who the second sitter would be. I know Lisa pretty well, so I felt I could be honest with her. "Lisa," I said, "Mary Anne, Dawn, Claudia and I have all got permission to go. Now we're trying to work out which one of us will take the job."

"Oh," Lisa said. "That sounds to me as if maybe *all* of you want to go."

"Something like that," I told her.

Lisa was silent for a second, then said, "I wonder if it wouldn't be more fun for the kids, and for the sitters, if all four of you came. It could be a holiday for everyone that way. The mansion is huge, so there's plenty of room. Instead of paying you, you'd get an all-expenses-paid trip to Maine. What do you think?"

I grinned at the others. They were still angry with me for my "I'm-the-chairman" outburst, and they wouldn't smile back. I couldn't blame them. I'd been pretty obnoxious.

I told Lisa, "I think that's a great idea. Let me talk to the others and I'll call you right back."

When I told everyone Lisa's idea, Dawn, Mary Anne and Claudia began hugging and hooting. Suddenly Mary Anne stopped and said, "But what about all the babysitting jobs we've lined up here?"

"Jessi and I can take a lot of them," Mal said eagerly. "Just leave the BSC to us." They actually looked happy about the idea of getting rid of us. I suppose we hadn't been much fun lately.

Logan put an arm round Mary Anne. "I hate the thought of you going away for ten days, Mary Anne," he said. "But I know how much you want to go to Reese. So I'll take over as many of the jobs as I can."

"Me too," Shannon said. "I could do with the money."

The meeting ran overtime, but we managed to come up with a schedule that freed Claudia, Mary Anne, Dawn and me for a two-week working holiday in Reese, Maine.

We were going to leave the next morning. That was barely enough time for Claudia to pack!

Mary Anne

Saturday Night
11 P.M.

I'm settled in my room in
historic Randolph mansion.
This is the first entry in
the BSC Reese Notebook.
Kristy, I thought Watson's
mansion was big. This
place is gigantic. Even with
sixteen people staying
here, there's one whole floor
we're not using!

Dawn, I didn't want to
admit it, but you're right
about this place feeling
haunted.

24

On Saturday morning Dawn and I woke up at seven o'clock. We were going to Maine and we still had packing to do. We ran to and fro between each other's rooms with questions such as: "Are you taking your navy stretch pants?" (Dawn to me); "Should I take trainers *and* sandals?" (me to Dawn); and, "Do you think I should pack my cowboy boots?" (Dawn to me). At one point— actually mid-way between our rooms— we bumped into one another as we asked in unison, "How many T-shirts are you bringing?"

At a quarter to ten, Sharon (who's Dawn's mother and my stepmother) dropped us off at the Engles' house. We hugged her goodbye. (We'd said goodbye to my dad earlier.) A van was parked in the drive. Seth had rented it so he could drive eight of us to Maine. Extra expenses such as this were one of the reasons we weren't getting paid for sitting.

As Sharon drove off, Seth and Lisa came out of their house lugging suitcases.

"Do you want some help?" Dawn asked.

"If you could go round the back and collect Andrew and Karen," Lisa said, "we can manage this."

Dawn and I walked around the house to the back garden. We could hear Karen and Andrew discussing the seating arrangements for the journey. "You can sit next to Claudia," Karen said.

"Kristy, too," Andrew said. "I want to sit with Kristy *and* Claudia."

"But I want to sit between Kristy and Mary Anne," Karen told him. "We can't fit five in a seat."

Andrew looked up and saw us. "Dawn, Kristy, Claudia *and* Mary Anne," he shouted. "I want to sit next to all of them."

"You can't, Andrew!" Karen yelled back. "It's impossible!"

Dawn and I exchanged a smile. Karen can be so precocious (that means bright for her age).

"Hi, you two," Dawn said. "Isn't this a perfect day for a journey?"

"We've got four babysitters," Andrew said as he jumped up and ran over to us. "One—two—three—four."

"Yes," I said. "And you can take turns sitting with each of us during the journey. How about that?"

"Yeah!" Andrew shouted as he ran off to tell his mother the good news.

As soon as we were in the front garden again, Claudia and Kristy arrived in Charlie's car. Claudia's suitcase was so big and heavy that it took Charlie *and* Kristy to carry it. The rest of us were wearing ordinary shorts and T-shirts for travelling, but not Claud. She had on a pair of bright blue Lycra cycling shorts, a black lacy tank top, a man's white dress shirt, baggy purple and

Mary Anne

white checked socks, red high-top trainers and a pair of big gold hoop earrings with a brightly-coloured wooden parrot perched on each hoop. She was carrying this gigantic bright yellow plastic beach bag stuffed with junk food for the trip.

"Hi, everybody," Claudia called out. "I hope we're not late. My parents took ages to say goodbye. You'd think we were going away for ever."

Kristy, weighed down with her end of Claudia's suitcase, mumbled, "I wonder where they got that idea. Could it be because you packed everything you own?"

"Claudia," Dawn teased, "we're _visiting_ Reese, not moving there."

At ten-thirty we were all finally buckled into the van and ready to begin what should have been a six-hour plus drive to Reese, Maine. For us, the "plus" ended up being an extra three and a half hours. One hour for lunch at a motorway café, one hour for getting lost, and one and a half hours for a picnic supper.

Even with my trusty guidebook of historical New England towns and Lisa's detailed road map, we took a wrong turning that detoured us through part of Vermont. I was quite glad, though, because it meant that on our way to Reese, Maine, we went through charming historic villages in four New England states:

27

Mary Anne

Connecticut, Massachusetts, New Hampshire *and* Vermont. Before we reached each town I read aloud from the guidebook. So as we were driving through, we already knew about the town's history, current and past industries, tourist attractions, and even the names of the best places to eat and sleep.

I might have got a bit carried away. Once, as we were zipping along on a motorway that bypassed a number of historic towns, Lisa said, "Mary Anne, I think the children might get more out of that book if you stuck to the towns we actually pass through and didn't read about the ones we're not even seeing."

I looked around the van. Next to me, in the middle seat, Kristy and Andrew were leaning against each other. They were sound alseep. In the back seat, Claudia and Karen were playing cat's cradle and humming "The Bear Went Over the Mountain". Dawn was listening to her Walkman. I'd pretty much lost my audience anyway.

I was staring out of the window and feeling bad about boring everyone to death, when Seth asked, "Mary Anne, where should we stop for a picnic?"

I flipped to the handy index in the back of the guidebook and looked up state parks. I found one that didn't take us too far out of our way. I was glad we ate our supper picnic-style. It gave everybody a chance to run around and burn off

28

some of the excess energy we'd stored up from being in the van all day.

But finding the park, eating and clearing up took a lot of time. So it was late when our van passed through the gates of the Randolph estate. Even though it was dark, we could see the mansion—white and massive—on top of the hill at the end of the winding driveway.

"Wow!" was all I could say. We were amazed by the size of the mansion. It was four storeys high, with a six-columned entranceway. Five brick chimneys pierced the cloudy night sky. And there was an authentic widow's walk on the roof.

"Look," Claudia said. "It's got a deck on the top. How strange."

"That's a widow's walk," I explained.

"Why is it called that?" Karen asked.

"Because that's where a woman went to watch for her husband's return from long whaling trips. She could get a good view of the sea from up there."

"Then how come it isn't called the 'wife's walk'?" Karen asked.

Before I could answer, Karen came up with the answer herself. "Oh, I know," she said. "Because sometimes the boat sank and the husband drowned in the sea and no one knew yet. So the woman walking up there was a widow, but she didn't know it yet. That *is* sad."

I told you Karen was precocious.

Mary Anne

As we tumbled out of the van, Mr and Mrs Menders hurried outside to greet us. Behind them I could see the Menders kids standing in the brightly-lit front hall of the mansion.

We unloaded our things and brought them inside.

Mr and Mrs Menders were really glad to see Seth and Lisa. And Karen and Andrew had met the Menders kids before, so they weren't total strangers.

When we'd dropped our luggage in the hall, Mr Menders said, "Let's all sit around the table in the dining room. We'll have some lemonade and make introductions in there." As we followed the Menders family into the dining room, I thought that they seemed rather lost in the big place.

We took seats at one end of the huge dining room table. (I'm going to stop saying *massive*, *huge* and *big*. Trust me, everything in this place—except the people—was oversized.) When we had passed around the lemonade, Mr Menders said, "Why don't we go around the table and introduce ourselves. Say your name and something about yourself. That'll help the sitters get to know the kids and vice versa." I decided that Mr Menders must be a corporate business type who was used to running meetings.

Jason, who's nine, introduced himself by saying, "I'm Jason. How come if there are four

sitters, and there are four of us, and two of us are
boys, two of you aren't boys, too?"

Lionel, who's fourteen (and too old to need a
sitter) said to his parents, "I'm not sure why
we've got a gaggle of sitters in the first place. We
don't need help to work out that Reese is a
nowhere place to be. I mean, the house is fine, but
the town's *nothing*."

"Actually," I began, "Reese was once—"

Dawn kicked me under the table. I realized she
was telling me to be quiet. It probably wasn't
the best time to begin a historical lecture about
Reese.

"We've already discussed this, Lionel," his
mother said. "Your father and I think you could
do with some company this holiday. The girls are
your age. They'll help you meet other kids."

Lionel sighed and said, "Whatever."

My instant assessment of Lionel Menders was:
pretentious and unhappy. He may not have
needed a babysitter, but it was clear to me that he
could do with some friends, and a change of
attitude.

"I think Reese will be lots of fun," ten-year-old
Jill said. I noticed that she had moved her chair
close to Dawn's. Then I noticed something else:
When we arrived, Jill's hair had been in a long
plait down her back. Now, her hair was draped
loosely over her shoulders, just like Dawn's. She
listed her likes and dislikes. Likes: swimming,

dressing up, dancing, summer, teenagers. Dislikes: people who act like babies, winter, being bored.

Martha, a seven-year-old, introduced herself by saying her name. That was all. OK. She was shy. And being a shy person myself, I could tell that Martha was rather overwhelmed by Karen's bubbly, outgoing personality. I overheard Karen tell her, "We're going to have so much fun. I'm great at meeting new people. You'll be the most popular person in Reese in no time at all."

"I don't know," Martha said meekly. "I miss Boston."

Next the babysitters and the adults introduced themselves. (I was right about Tom Menders being a corporate businessman.) When the introductions were finished, Mr Menders told us, "You'll meet Mr and Mrs Cooper in the morning. They'll be preparing our meals, cleaning up and generally being helpful."

My friends and I exchanged a glance. A mansion with a caretaker couple! Even if the kids were going to be a challenge, we were going to be taken care of, food-wise and otherwise. We were used to babysitting jobs for which we had to do everything.

"Of course," Mrs Menders said, "as there are so many of us, we'll all be pitching in."

"Of course," Kristy said.

"But when it comes to household matters,"

Mrs Menders continued, "the Coopers are in charge."

"Did they come with the mansion?" Kristy asked.

"No," Mr Menders said, "we've just hired them for the summer. But if we decide to stay, we hope they will, too. They've already proved themselves very helpful. They're quite charming and have lived here since they were young."

"Don't forget that little matter of Mrs Cooper's voice," Lionel put in.

"What?" Dawn asked.

Lionel began speaking in the deep, accented voice of a horror movie narrator. "Mrs Cooper doesn't ha-ave a vo-oice. She's afflicted with chronic laryngitis. There may be permanent injury to her vocal cords. Ve-ry sta-range."

Lionel put on a menacing expression to match the scary voice he was using.

"Oh, Lionel," Jill said matter-of-factly, "stop it!"

"Lionel's always trying out different characters," Jason said by way of explanation. "He's going to be an actor."

"I *am* an actor, my dear boy," Lionel said. "Please, be precise." (Now he was impersonating a rich English gentleman.)

"Well, everyone," Mr Menders said, "it's gone ten. Let's put the girls in the west wing and call it a night, shall we?"

Mary Anne

We carried our luggage (Mr Menders helped Claudia) up the wide marble staircase and down a long corridor, through a doorway that led to another set of stairs, that led to the second-floor landing. We and our charges would occupy eight bedrooms opening onto the corridor—four on each side. "OK," Mr Menders said. "Your first job is to decide who sleeps where. Our kids will tell you which rooms they've already claimed."

We did a lot of shuffling around and discussing, but at last we settled on the following allocation of rooms.

Facing East	Facing West
Kristy and Andrew	Dawn
bath (connecting)	(connecting door)
Mary Anne	Claudia
Karen and Martha	Jason
(connecting door)	(connecting door)
Jill	Lionel
Bath	Locked door to fourth floor stairs

By the time we'd worked out our room arrangements, Lionel and Jason were already in their rooms with the doors closed. I took Martha and Karen to their room and put them to sleep with a story. When I came back onto the landing I

34

saw that Jill was sleepily trailing Dawn. ("I'll go to sleep when you do, Dawn.")

I went back to my own room and looked around. I don't think the second floor of the west wing had been used for a *very* long time. The Coopers had done their best to dust and air everything. And the beds were made up with fresh sheets. But I had this eerie feeling that I'd gone back in time. As I took in the details of the room I imagined another girl—a hundred years earlier—touching the very same curtain, seeing her reflection in the same mirror, sleeping in the same bed. A shiver ran up my spine. I was glad my friends and I had decided to leave the doors to the corridor and between our rooms open while we unpacked and got ready for bed.

I studied the headboard of the bed. It was decorated with a night view of a stormy sea and a lighthouse. A painted shaft of light beamed from the lighthouse across the painted sea.

When I'd put my clothes away I opened my casement window and looked out over the Atlantic Ocean. I could hear its roar and feel the moist, salty breeze on my face. I noticed a moving beam of light playing over the sea. "Kristy," I called. "Come here."

Claudia, Dawn, Kristy and Jill ran into my room. We stood at my window watching as the rough sea was illuminated section by section. "A

35

lighthouse," I explained, "just like the one painted on my headboard."

"This place feels weird to me," Dawn whispered. "I bet it's haunted."

"Come on, Dawn," I whispered back. "Don't start. We need a good night's sleep if we're going to be babysitting all day tomorrow."

Just then I felt a furry mass brush against my leg. I shrieked. The furry mass jumped on my bed, arched its back, and hissed at me. It was a black cat with green eyes. I screamed again. This time Claudia, Dawn and Kristy joined in.

But Jill said, "Oh, there you are, Spooky." She walked towards the cat. "You scared my new friends."

"Is that *your* cat?" Dawn asked Jill. (I was still speechless with fright.)

"Sort of," Jill answered. "It was already here when we came. I suppose it was Great-Uncle Randolph's."

Spooky let Jill pick him up, but his eyes were still trained on me. I love cats. I do. But a black one, slinking out of nowhere?

"OK, Jill," Dawn said. "It's definitely time for bed. I'll read you a story."

When Dawn, Jill and Spooky had left, I said, "I think I'll close my door."

"Me, too," said Claud as she darted across the landing.

Kristy and I decided to leave the doors between

36

our rooms open and she went back to her bedroom. I slid between the clean sheets and tried to calm down by writing in our Reese Notebook. (The BSC notebook was back in Stoneybrook with Mal and Jessi.)

When I'd finished my notebook entry and turned off my lamp, I lay in bed listening to the creaks and groans of the mansion. I couldn't close my eyes, much less sleep. I told myself that of course there are creaks and groans. This is a windy night, in a very old house that isn't used to having so many people in it. That was when I saw a flickering light under the door to the landing. At first I thought it must be the beam from the lighthouse, but then I realized the lighthouse didn't shine *in* the house. Flicker. Flicker. There it was again.

I lay stiffly in bed, hardly breathing. I was afraid if I stayed alone in my room my heart would *burst* with fright. The doors between my room and Kristy's were still open. I took a deep breath, jumped out of bed, and flew through the bathroom to Kristy's room. She was sitting up in bed, staring at the door to *her* room. Andrew was asleep, so I whispered, "Did you see that?"

Kristy nodded.

"Maybe someone turned on the hall light, and the bulb's nearly burned out, so it's flickering," I suggested.

"It looks like candlelight," Kristy said.

Mary Anne

"*Ohh—ohh.*" We heard a low ghostly moan in the hall. "*Oh-hh.*"

I grabbed Kristy.

We sat there holding our breath—and each other—as we stared at the door. Then, as suddenly as they had begun, the flickering light went out and the moaning ended.

Silence.

"Do you think Claud and Dawn heard that?" Kristy asked.

"I don't know," I said. "But I'm not going over there to find out."

I spent the night in Kristy's room. By the time I fell asleep, I wasn't so sure that I was glad to be in the historic seaside town of Reese, Maine.

4th CHAPTER

Dawn

Sunday
5:00 p.m.

Kristy, I know you're afraid that if we get caught up in this haunted house thing, the Menders kids won't want to move to Reese. But how can we keep the kids from noticing the strange things that are happening in their mansion?

By the way, everyone keep an eye on Georgio. I don't trust him.

Dawn

"Listen, you lot," Kristy said, "if this is such a big house, why are we all crowded into one little bathroom?"

It was seven-thirty on our first morning in Reese, and Kristy, Claud, Mary Anne and I were brushing our teeth in what was probably the only small room in the mansion—the bathroom between Kristy and Mary Anne's rooms.

As I brushed my teeth, my elbow caught Kristy in the neck. "Sorry," I gurgled.

"There *is* another bathroom just down the corridor," Kristy commented.

"Claud and I heard and saw some pretty weird things last night—" Rinse. Rinse. Spit. Spit. —"in that corridor," I said.

In the mirror I saw a Look pass between Mary Anne and Kristy. I guessed they'd seen and heard some pretty weird things, too. Then we were all talking at once, comparing notes on the ghost.

"Maybe it was our imaginations," Mary Anne said. "You know, because we're in a strange place and everything."

"But we all imagined the *same thing*," I replied. "That's called 'evidence', not 'imagination'."

A sleepy voice accompanied a knock on the bathroom door. "Dawn, are you in there?"

It was Jill. Kristy put a finger to her lips as we exchanged a Look, silently agreeing not to talk about ghostly matters in front of the Menders kids.

"I'll be right out, Jill," I said.

"What are you going to wear today, Dawn?" Jill asked.

We stifled giggles.

"Shorts and a T-shirt," I answered. "Over my swimsuit. See you at breakfast."

Breakfast was set out on the side verandah, a huge wooden-pillared porch that ran along the side of the house. It was a perfect, clear-skied, warm summer day. The mansion and its grounds were even more impressive in daylight than at night. And *much* less scary.

Cereals, bananas, fresh strawberries, yoghurt juice and milk were laid out on a sideboard. We served ourselves and sat down around a big wooden table. When Mrs Cooper appeared with a basket of homemade blueberry muffins, Mrs Menders introduced her to us. Mrs Cooper was younger than I expected—probably about my mother's age—and very pretty, with straight dark hair pulled back in a bun. But Lionel was right, she didn't talk. She had a nice smile, though.

As I ate a bowl of fresh strawberries and yoghurt, I looked out at the beautiful estate gardens and the sea beyond. I was thinking about the ghostly apparition of the night before and wondering what ghosts did during the day. Suddenly a deep, ominous voice murmured in my ear, "Sleep well last night, my pretty?"

Dawn

I shrieked and practically jumped out of my skin.

"Lionel!" his mother said sharply, "That is *not* funny."

Lionel looked around at us sitters and asked in his horror-movie voice, "Ev-very-one get a go-od night's sleep?"

"Just eat your breakfast, Lionel," Mr Menders said. "You kids can go to the beach today, if you want. The Coopers will pack you a picnic lunch. Tonight we'll have a barbecue. And, Lionel, behave yourself."

"Yes, sir. Right, sir." (That was Lionel as a soldier.) Lionel was as annoying with his so-called acting as my brother Jeff is with his so-called comedy routines.

Luckily, all the kids agreed that they wanted to go to the beach. (Lionel: "I'll go along. If anybody is anybody around here they'll probably be there." Jason: "Of course. Why not?" Jill: "Is that what you're going to do, Dawn?" Martha: "OK. I suppose." Karen: "Great. There'll be lots of kids for Martha to meet at the beach." Andrew: "Can I look for frogs? Can I?")

The adults made sure we knew the way to the beach, and gave us some beach rules to follow with their kids. We decided that, for the morning at least, Claud and I would be responsible for Karen, Martha and—as she was practically glued to me anyway—Jill. Kristy and Mary Anne would look after Andrew and Jason. Lionel, of course, could do whatever he wanted, which I was sure would include pestering us.

While everyone else was finishing breakfast and clearing the table, Claud and I went up to the second floor of the west wing to make our beds and pack some beach things. The moment we were away from the others, Claud and I started talking about the ghost.

"Let's check the corridor for evidence," Claud said.

First we turned the corridor light on and off a few times. No flickers. It worked perfectly. "The light we saw under the door looked like candlelight, anyway," Claud said. "It had a yellowy glow. The bulb in the corridor light fixture gives off a pink glow."

I dropped to my hands and knees. "Let's look for wax. Candles and dripping wax go together."

"I don't know if a ghost's candle would drip," Claud said.

"What's that?" I asked, pointing to a small dark-orange blob on the carpet.

Claud knelt down and rubbed the spot with her finger. "Wax," she said. "And here's another spot."

And there were more. Not big blobs of wax, but fine little flecks of it here and there, all the way down the corridor.

Dawn

Suddenly a booming, sinister voice asked, "What are you do-o-ing?"

I was startled and afraid. Still, I looked up. Lionel was standing over us.

"Why are you crawling around on the floor?" he asked in his natural voice.

"Dawn dropped the back of an earring," Claud said.

I stood up. "Well, it's no big deal. Let's go to the beach."

"If it's not a big deal why did you look in the first place?" Lionel asked as he swung around and went into his room.

Claud and I exchanged a look. "What's the matter with him?" I asked in a whisper.

"Maybe he knows something about the wax on the carpet," Claud said. "Maybe he's our ghost."

I nodded. Lionel was a strong suspect.

During the next half an hour we made beds and helped the kids pack for the beach. Then we set off down the long drive towards the gate. We must have been a sight—ten kids of all ages loaded with picnic baskets, beach toys, towels, etc. Maybe that's why the dark, handsome guy we saw walking towards us was smiling. Or was he laughing? It was hard to tell, because he was wearing reflective sunglasses.

Here's what the stranger looked like—one of those brooding teenage rebel loners. A sinister one, with his black T-shirt, black jeans and those sunglasses. But it wasn't the clothes that made him seem sinister as much as his looks. He had straight black hair, heavy eyebrows and a crooked smile.

"Hi," he said when he reached us.

"Hi," we all answered.

He'd stopped, so we did too.

"Can we help you?" the efficient Kristy asked.

"I work here," he said. Just as I was thinking I wished he'd take off his sunglasses so I could see his eyes, he did. They were dark brown and alight with interest. Or was that an evil glint? The guy was really hard to read.

"You must be the Menders kids," he said. "I didn't know there were so many of you. Good thing the house is big."

There was that crooked smile again. Was it sinister or friendly? He was making me nervous.

"I'm Georgio Trono," he said as he extended a hand to shake with Claudia.

"I'm Claudia Kishi," she replied. "And we don't all live here. Some of us are babysitting for the—" Claud gestured around at the younger kids—"others." I could tell she was flustered, especially when Georgio's handshake lasted a few seconds longer than a handshake should. Georgio, whether he was friendly or not, was definitely a flirt. And he was flirting with Claud.

Kristy took care of the rest of the introductions. Then Georgio told us that his grandparents had been the caretakers of the mansion when Mr Randolph was alive. "They're retired now," he explained, "but I'm still the summer gardener here. I practically lived here when I was a kid. What rooms are you lot staying in?"

We told him the west wing of the second floor and I mentioned that the house was so big we hadn't even been on the third floor yet.

Georgio's smile disappeared. "Don't go up there!" he said in a firm voice.

"Why not?" Claud asked.

"For one thing, the widow's walk isn't safe," he said. "And there's bats and . . ." He paused before adding, ". . . who knows what else in the attic."

I felt a chill run down my spine. No one said anything for a second.

Georgio smiled again. "But don't let that ruin your holiday. Reese is a great place."

We let out a collective sigh of relief and said goodbye. Georgio kept going towards the mansion, and we headed for the gate.

"Wow!" Mary Anne whispered to me. "Did you see the way he looked at Claud?"

We ran to Claud who was walking between Karen and Martha. "Karen and Martha, why don't you race to the gate?" I suggested. "We'll carry your things."

As soon as Karen and Martha were "on your marks, get set, gone," Mary Anne and I both asked Claud what she had thought about the mysterious Georgio.

"He's a Babe," Claud said. "But I've got an uneasy feeling about him. I wonder why he doesn't want us to go to the third floor?"

"And why is he so interested in what rooms we're staying in?" Mary Anne asked.

"He gives me the creeps," I said. "I can't explain it, but I don't trust him."

"Me neither," Claud said. But I noticed that she was looking dreamy, and was gently rubbing the palm of the hand Georgio had shaken.

When we got to the beach we put Georgio out of our minds and concentrated on getting our blankets laid out and the kids coated with sunblock. Just being on a beach, any beach, reminds me of California and makes me feel homesick for my life there. That's been happening to me more and more lately—missing California, I mean.

Lionel put on his sunglasses and checked out the beach for any "actor-types". In ten minutes he gave us his evaluation. "Only conservative, family types. No one sophisticated. No one hip. No one cool. Reese is one big fat no-place. I'll see you all back at the mansion." Oh, no. Were we losing Lionel so quickly? We were supposed to be helping him adjust.

"Come on, Lionel," I said. "Don't go away. It's a bit early for the hip crowd. In California, nobody who's anybody turns up at the beach before midday. Have a little patience."

"How do you know what they do in California?" he asked.

Mary Anne and Kristy answered in unison, "She's *from* California!"

Lionel's face lit up. "You are?"

When I told him I'd grown up in California and lived there most of my life, he sat down next to me.

Lionel asked me dozens of questions about California and the Hollywood movie scene. Luckily, I had had a lot of actor sightings. And, as the father of one of my best California friends is a film producer, I'd even met a few famous actors. Lionel was thrilled.

"Gosh!" Lionel said. "Why couldn't Uncle Edward have had a mansion in L.A.? I'd have moved there in an instant!"

While we were talking, Mary Anne was building a sand castle with Karen and Martha, and Andrew was burying Kristy's feet and legs in sand. I saw Karen introduce herself to two girls who she then brought over to work on the sand castle. But Martha, meanwhile, stood up and walked to the edge of the water. She was pretending, as far as I could tell, that she didn't know Karen. Mary Anne signalled me to take over at the sand castle while she talked to Martha. I excused myself from Lionel's company and

48

approached Karen and her new "friends".

I could hear Karen telling the other girls, "You'll love Martha. She's so much fun." Then Karen called out, "Come on, Martha, build with us. Everyone wants to meet you."

Poor shy Martha, I thought. This isn't what she needs. While Mary Anne took Martha's hand and walked down the beach with her, I squatted next to Karen. (In a flash, Jill was right there beside me.) "Can we help?" I asked Karen.

"OK," she answered.

"Great," I said. I played with them for a while, but the sea was beckoning. "I'll be right back," I said.

Jill, who an instant before had seemed extremely enthusiastic about sand castle building, stood up too. "Where are you going?" she asked as she brushed the sand off her knees. "I want to do whatever the *teenagers* do." I'd been thinking that if Jill were working on the sand castle it would be easier for Martha to join in later. Forget it! Jill was going for a swim with me. Which meant I couldn't go out as far as I wanted. Or even have two minutes to myself to think about the haunted house and the orange wax, or to wonder about Georgio.

Meanwhile, Jason was sitting alone on his towel. He'd moved himself farther down the beach, so as not to look as if he were at the beach with seven girls. I waved to him. "Come on, Jason. We're going for a swim."

He shook his head glumly and lay down. Lionel, who was now reading a book of plays, ignored his little brother. He didn't even seem to notice—or care—that Jason was isolating himself from the rest of us.

Once again I realized that while the Menders kids were all perfectly nice, sitting for them wasn't going to be easy.

After a swim in the sea, more sand castle building and a terrific picnic lunch courtesy of the Coopers, Claud suggested we pack up our things and go for a walk through town.

By then Lionel had given up on finding the in-crowd at Reese beach and gone back to the mansion. The rest of us made for the shops and restaurants lining the streets near the harbour. Kristy spotted a sports goods shop and steered Jason in that direction. "We'll catch up with you later," she told the rest of us.

We went into a T-shirt shop that sold just the kinds of souvenirs we wanted. I noticed a big community notice board. "Let's look at that," I suggested. "We might find some ideas for things we can do with the kids."

"There's an announcement about the historical society," Mary Anne said, "Right here in town."

Claud said, "And look at this." She pointed to a big blue and white poster. "Reese is celebrating its two hundred and fiftieth birthday. Founders' Day. There's going to be a parade with floats."

"And a carnival and rides and everything," Karen said. "Goody!"

"It's next Saturday," I added. "We'll still be here."

By then Kristy and Jason had joined us. Kristy was beaming, which meant that the trip to the sports shop had been good for Jason. "I got a new softball," he told us.

We showed Kristy the poster for Founders' Day. "Uh-oh!" Kristy said. I had a feeling she was remembering a few other times when Claud had persuaded us to dress up for parades. The members of the BSC have gone to some outrageous extremes to provide Claud with opportunities to express her artistic talent.

Claud told the younger kids how much fun it would be to dress up and be in a parade together.

Karen jumped up and down and shouted, "Hurray! We're going to ride on a float. Everybody will see us."

Martha just stood there shaking her head no. "Maybe Martha could help me with the research, and make the costumes," Mary Anne said. Then she whispered to Martha, just loudly enough for us to hear, "I don't like being in parades either."

"I'll be in it if Dawn is," Jill said. (So what else was new?)

"Maybe we could make a historical float,"

Dawn

Mary Anne mused, "as we're in historical New England and it's a historical celebration."

Jason was reading every single announcement on the notice board. "What's summer stock?" he asked. "Is that like stock car racing? I'd go to the stock car races, I mean if there were some boys to go with."

We gathered around him to read the poster that had caught his attention. "Summer stock is theatrical productions put on during the summer," I explained. "You know, plays."

"You find summer stock in tourist areas, like historic New England," Mary Anne added.

"Oh," said Jason. He sounded disappointed.

"The play that's on while we're here is *Dracula*," Kristy said.

"Just what we need," Claud said with a shiver. "Something scary."

"But maybe it's just what Lionel needs," I said. I was getting an idea. "Lionel thinks there aren't any actors around here," I continued. "But this actor, the one who plays Count Dracula, is famous. Not like a leading, leading man. But his name's always in the newspapers in L.A., for one thing or another. I bet Lionel will recognize it."

Mary Anne wrote down the actor's name, the dates and times of the performances, and the price of the tickets. She'd also taken careful note of the days and times the historical society was open, and the details for Founders' Day. That's our Mary Anne—BSC secretary.

As we made our way back to the mansion with our troop of kids, I felt pretty good about our first day in Reese. It was the night-time I was worried about. And, as it turned out, I had good reason to worry about it.

5th CHAPTER

Jessi

Today's special meeting of the BSC went great. We notified clients about our reassigned jobs, and took on some new ones besides. I hope the Reese division of the BSC is having a fun vacation knowing that the club is in good hands.

Jessi

"Let's take turns being acting chairman," Mal said. "You go first, and I'll be secretary."

It was one o'clock on Sunday and Mal and I were conducting a special meeting of the BSC. The meeting was held in Claudia's room, of course. I loved it. I, Jessi Ramsey, age eleven, was acting chairman of the Babysitters Club. I sat in Kristy's director's chair and put on her visor. Mal lay across Claud's bed with the record book in front of her. So far there were only two people attending the meeting—us.

We knew that Logan wouldn't be there, because he was working the Sunday brunch shift at the Rosebud Cafe. But he had given Mal his work schedule for the next ten days so we'd know when he was free to babysit. "Just phone and let me know when you need me," he said. He's a really nice guy. No wonder Mary Anne likes him so much.

The other person who was supposed to be attending the meeting was Shannon, of course. But she hadn't arrived yet.

When she finally walked in at 1:14 I said, "This meeting of the Babysitters Club—"

"Hey, you two," Shannon said, "don't you even say hello?"

Mal and I both said hello to her. Shannon sat on Claud's desk and said, "My dad's picking me up here at one-thirty so we'd better get started."

Mal and I exchanged a glance. Who was

55

running this meeting anyway? Shannon would *never* act that way if Kristy were sitting in the director's chair.

I sat tall and said, "This is a special meeting of the Babysitters Club. The first order of business is to phone clients to tell them they're getting a different sitter from the one they were originally assigned." I turned to secretary Mallory and asked, "Who shall we ring first?"

"The Kuhns," she answered. "They're expecting Kristy tomorrow at ten. You're taking her place."

Jake Kuhn answered the phone. I told him that Kristy had an out-of-town job and I would be sitting for him, Laurel and Patsy the next day.

"That's awful," he moaned.

"What?" I asked. "What's awful?"

"I want Kristy to sit. She said she'd practise softball with me."

"I know how to play softball," I told him.

"But Kristy's my coach. She was going to teach me how to throw a knuckleball. Do you know how to throw a knuckleball?"

I had to tell him that I didn't. I'd have to think of something extra-special to do with Jake.

My next phone call was to the Kormans. Melody wasn't any happier than Jake was about having a substitute sitter. "I was going to ask Mary Anne to teach me how to make doll's clothes," she complained.

"Mallory can help you make up stories about your dolls," I suggested.

"But my dolls haven't got any clothes!" Melody whined.

I made sure to tell Mal that Melody wanted to make doll's clothes. Knowing Mal, she'd come up with some nifty ideas for dressing dolls before she babysat for Melody.

I made three more calls to clients explaining substitutions. Luckily those calls went a little better than my first two.

When I'd finished the last call Shannon asked, "Have you listened to the messages on the answering machine?"

"That's what we're doing next," I said. I didn't tell her that I'd forgotten about the answering machine. It's a good thing Shannon thought of it, because the Prezziosos, the Arnolds and the Hobarts had all called needing sitters.

I called Mrs Prezzioso first. She said she needed two sitters for Monday afternoon. "My sister-in-law and her twins are visiting," she explained. "They're two-year-old boys and of course there's Jenny and the baby."

"OK," I said, "we'll call you right back."

We checked our schedules. I was sitting for the Kuhns all day. Logan was working at the Rosebud Cafe. Shannon was sitting at my house for Becca and Squirt.

"I can handle the job alone," Mal said, "if Mrs

Jessi

Prezzioso doesn't mind. I look after my brothers. Twins will be a piece of cake after triplets."

I called Mrs Prezzioso back and she agreed. "Just warn Mallory," Mrs Prezzioso said, "that my nephews are a handful."

The next call was to Mrs Hobart. She needed a sitter for Wednesday night. Logan was working at the Rosebud, but Shannon was free and she said she'd take the job.

A horn honked outside the Kishis' house. "Uh-oh!" Shannon said. "It's one-thirty. And there's my lift. Gotta go." As she was leaving she added, "Next time let's try to end on time." She walked out of the room.

"How about *starting* on time?" I mumbled.

Shannon poked her head back into the room. Had she heard me? "You two," she said, "don't be discouraged. You're doing a great job. Sorry I was late today."

"That's OK," I said. "See you Monday at—" —"five thirty," we said in unison.

"But I can't make it," Shannon said. "That's what I came back to tell you. I'll leave you a message on the machine about when I can sit."

When Shannon had gone we called the Arnolds. They needed a sitter for Monday night at seven-thirty for Carolyn and Marilyn. "I'll call you right back," I told Mrs Arnold.

"Shannon's already sitting," Mal said. "And neither of us can do it because it's at night. But on

Jessi

Monday Logan finishes work at the Rosebud at six-thirty, so he can probably start a sitting job at seven-thirty. Tell Mrs Arnold that Logan will sit."

"Shouldn't we call Logan first?" I asked.

"He said not to call him at work," Mal reminded me. "I'll call and tell him later."

I phoned Mrs Arnold again and told her Logan would be there at seven-thirty on Monday night.

"Thank goodness," she said. "Mr Arnold and I are hosting the auction for Stoneybrook Ambulance Services. I don't know what I would have done if I couldn't find a sitter."

"I'm glad we can help, Mrs Arnold," I said.

I felt pretty good when I rang off. The BSC was an important part of the community. And Mal and I were running it.

"This meeting of the Babysitters Club is adjourned," I told Mallory in a deep-voiced, serious tone.

She broke into giggles. I did too. As we were leaving Claudia's room Mal said, "That was a great meeting, chairman."

I looked at my watch. "Uh-oh!" I said, "I'd better get a move on. I've got a job at the Mancusis' in ten minutes."

As I ran down the street I wondered how things were going for the Reese division of the BSC.

6th CHAPTER

Kristy

Sunday night
10:00 p.m.

Tonight I caught the "ghost" in the act. Unfortunately, it seems he's not the only one. Ghost, I mean. Guys, we have to be extra careful not to let on to the rest of the Menders kids that there are some _very_ _weird_ things going on in their new home. They're having enough trouble getting into the swing of things in Reese.

Sunday night was a perfect night for a barbecue. Elton Cooper grilled burgers, hot dogs and chicken for us. After spending most of the day outside, at the beach and in town, we had big appetites. Elton isn't as friendly as his wife, which is strange as he can talk and she can't. But boy, does he know his barbecue!

After supper we were sitting around the verandah table, talking about Founders' Day.

"I think making a float is a great idea," Mrs Menders said.

Martha ran to her mother and whispered something in her ear. "But, of course, not everyone has to be *on* the float," Mrs Menders added.

"Martha and I are behind-the-scenes helpers," Mary Anne told the Menderses.

I could see that Karen was about to make a case for Martha's being on the float, so I said, "Karen, would you please go up to my room and find Andrew's *Frog and Toad* book?"

"If Martha will come with me," Karen said.

As the girls were leaving the porch I heard Karen tell Martha, "We could have a float about animals. You would make a perfect cat. Everyone loves cats. It would make you very popular."

"Dressing-up is for girls," Jason told whoever would listen. "I'm not going to be on any stupid float."

"Count me out," Lionel told Claudia. "It's too makeshift and unprofessional for me."

Claud always has trouble getting us psyched up for her parade floats. But the Menders kids were really going to be a challenge.

The adults announced that they wanted to go into town to see how busy the shops were in the evening, so I said we'd be happy to look after the kids.

When they'd gone, Dawn (and Jill) started a conversation with Lionel about the summer stock theatre while Claud and Mary Anne cleared the table. "Come on, Jason," Claud said. "Let's have a little help here."

"Oh, OK," Jason said. "I'll carry the heavy stuff for you."

When Karen and Martha got back, I moved to the edge of the verandah, where the porch light would fall on the pages of the book. Andrew climbed onto my lap. Martha and Karen sat on either side of me. *"Frog and Toad Together,"* I read from the cover, "by Arnold Lobel." I looked around at the kids. "This book has a lot of little stories in it. Shall I read them in the order they're in the book?"

"Yes," Martha said.

"Read them all," said Karen.

"Rib-bid," added Andrew.

By the time I got to the last story in the book, Karen was reading all Toad's lines and Lionel—

who was now standing behind me—was reading Frog's lines. (I hate to admit it, but he was good.) I did the narration. The others had finished carrying things back to the kitchen and were listening to us.

When I said "the end", Andrew looked up at me and said, "Kristy, I want to be a frog *and* a toad in the parade."

Karen said that Andrew couldn't be both a frog and a toad. That they were two different kinds of animals.

"Well, they're sort of alike," Jill said. "They both hop and live in ponds."

"Do they?" Andrew asked me.

"Toads live in the grass and under rocks," I said. "Frogs live in ponds. But I don't know much more than that."

Dawn went inside to find a dictionary. When she got back with one we looked up "frog" and "toad" and read the definitions out loud. Mary Anne pointed out that a frog's skin is smooth and moist while a toad's is rough and dry.

Andrew looked more curious than ever. "You know what, Andrew?" I said. "Let's go and *find* some frogs and toads and you can *see* the difference."

Elton Cooper, who was putting the cover on the grill, overheard us. "You'll find frogs in that little pond behind the old gardener's cottage," he said. "Go down the path that starts near the kitchen door and follow it through the pine grove. The cottage is back there. I'll bring you a torch."

Lionel decided to skip our "little excursion", as he called it. Jason said he was going to his room to organize his baseball cards. With Lionel promising to keep an eye on his younger brother, the rest of us were free to go on our frog and toad hunt.

I was glad Elton thought of the torch because it was a moonless, dark night. Once we were far away from the house we wouldn't have been able to see each other, much less toads and frogs.

We found a toad under a rock at the edge of the rose garden. "This toad is small," Andrew said.

"It's so sweet," Karen added. She did a terrific imitation of a toad's jump for Andrew.

I led everybody along the path Mr Cooper had described. It was pitch-black in the pine grove. When I turned to look back at the house, I thought that it looked . . . different. Mary Anne thought so, too. Her voice was trembling when she whispered in my ear, "Look. There's a light on. On the *top floor*. The one with the attic and the old servants' quarters. I thought nobody went up there." We stood still, staring at the mansion while Claud and Dawn continued walking with the kids.

Suddenly, the light went off and the top floor was dark again. What was going on? Who was up there?

"Come on, slow coaches," Claud called back to us.

Mary Anne and I caught up with the others in front of the gardener's cottage. "Isn't it lovely?" Claud said. She sounded cheerful, so I knew she hadn't seen the light. To me the cottage looked rather rundown and spooky.

"It would be fun to play in there," Karen said. "Can Martha and I use it for our playhouse?"

"It's too far from the main house," I told her. "Anyhow, you've got plenty of other things to do." I took Andrew by one hand and Karen by the other. With all these weird things going on, I wanted to keep the kids as close to me as possible.

The excursion was giving me the creeps. If it hadn't been for Andrew pulling on my hand and saying, "I want to see a frog," I would have turned back then.

We found the pond and, after a bit of searching, we found a frog, too. Then another. Andrew spoke in rib-bit language to both of them.

"OK, you lot," I said, "we've seen one toad and two frogs. Let's go back. It's late."

Dawn, Jill and Claud took the lead on the path. Mary Anne and I followed with Karen, Martha and Andrew. I glanced up at the house. A chill ran down my spine. The top-floor window was lit up again. Claud ran back to me. "Did you see that?" she whispered. She was pretty spooked too.

Especially as by the time we reached the back door, we'd seen it go out again.

It was a relief to get back into the big kitchen and Margaret Cooper's pleasant smile. Even gruff Elton's presence made me feel less frightened.

"Find any frogs?" he asked.

"Rib-bit, Rib-bit," Andrew answered.

We all laughed. Even Margaret. I suppose with some vocal cord problems you can still laugh.

"Yes, we did," I said as I handed Elton the torch. "Thanks for this."

"Let's go, kids," Dawn said. "I'll take you upstairs. It's bedtime."

"And storytime," Karen added.

"I'll come too," Mary Anne said.

"What can we do to help you in here, Mr Cooper?" Claud asked.

"You could count out the morning dishes and silverware," he said. "And please, call me Elton. And my wife's name is Margaret."

I thought again how nice the Coopers—Elton and Margaret—were, and what a long working day they'd had, with all the cooking and cleaning. I was glad to help them. And maybe they could help me, too . . . with the mystery.

While I was counting out spoons I casually asked Elton, "Does anybody ever go up to the top floor?"

"Oh, no," he said. "It hasn't been used in

years, maybe decades. I've never been up there myself."

"That's strange," Claud said. "When we were out just now we saw a light go on in one of the rooms in the west wing of the third floor."

"Off and on," I said. "First it was on. Then it was off. Then it went on again. And off."

"Couldn't be," Elton said. "The door to the stairway leading up there is locked. I've heard tell there were strange goings-on up there some years ago. That's probably when it was closed off."

"What kind of goings-on?" Claud asked.

Margaret Cooper rapped the kitchen worktop with a wooden spoon and shook her head no. I had a feeling she didn't want her husband to tell us what they knew about the top floor.

"It's nothing for your young ears to hear," he said. "Besides, that was then and this is now."

Margaret put her right arm out straight in front of herself and moved it in a circle.

"My wife thinks maybe it was the lighthouse light reflecting off the windows that you saw," Elton explained.

"Yeah," I said. "Maybe."

When we'd put our charges to sleep, the Reese contingent of the BSC met in Mary Anne's room. Andrew was already asleep in mine. My friends and I were seriously frightened.

Claud went to the window and looked out over

67

the sea. "There's no way the beam from the lighthouse could have reflected on that window," she told us. "We were looking at the back of the house. It's the *front* of the house that faces the ocean and the lighthouse."

"Maybe Lionel did it," Mary Anne said. "He was inside. Maybe he was checking out the third floor. It *is* his house."

It sounded as if Mary Anne was hoping with all her heart that Lionel was responsible for the light on the top floor. But I had to remind her, "Elton said the door to the staircase is locked and no one has a key."

"I know you lot don't want to admit this," Dawn said, "but the house *could* be haunted by ghosts. A ghost in the corridor last night. And one on the third floor tonight."

"Please, Dawn, don't say that," Mary Anne said. "There has to be an explanation."

"We did see that wax on the rug," Claud said.

"Who says a ghost can't use real candles?" Dawn asked.

Nobody had an answer for that. And as we weren't making any progress, we decided to make for our rooms. Dawn, Claudia and I had already stood up. Then we heard it again. "*Ohh-hh! Ohh-hh!*" This time it was a high-pitched and eerie voice. I leaned over and turned off Mary Anne's bedside lamp. We all stared at the slit under the door. Candlelight flickered there. My heart pounded. Maybe Dawn was right, and this house was haunted.

Then I had a hunch. There was no time to discuss it with the others. I drew in a deep breath, and tiptoed to the door. I almost turned back when I heard that "*ohh-hh, ohh-hh!*" again. But even though my heart was pounding practically out of my chest by then, I reached over, grabbed the knob and threw the door open.

My terrified friends gasped. I screeched. But a minute later, we were laughing. Because in the doorway stood a very startled "ghost"—Lionel.

"Oops!" he said. "You weren't supposed to do that. It wasn't in the script."

We were so relieved to have solved the mystery of the ghost in the corridor that we couldn't stop laughing. Even Lionel relaxed and laughed with us. By then we were standing in the hall.

"Very, very funny," Dawn said. "And the lights on the third floor tonight, Lionel. That was really good. You deserve the special effects Academy Award."

"What lights on the third floor?" Lionel asked.

"Lionel, we know you were up there turning the lights on and off," I said.

"I wouldn't go up there alone," he protested. "I'd be too afraid. Anyhow, the door's locked."

I didn't believe him. After all, he was an actor. Dawn didn't believe him either. "Lionel," she said, "if you don't confess right now, I'll never,

ever tell you another thing about Hollywood, not even the tiniest bit of gossip."

"That's not fair," Lionel said. "You lot are all crazy."

Just then I heard footsteps. Coming from upstairs. The others must have heard them, too, because everybody was looking up. And I had a feeling they were all thinking what I was thinking—upstairs is the third floor. The floor nobody can reach because the door is locked.

As good an actor as Lionel was, he couldn't have pretended the fear that drained the colour from his face. Claud, Mary Anne and I huddled close to one another. They looked as pale as Lionel. I was feeling a little faint and weak in the knees myself.

"Wha-at's tha-at?" Mary Anne managed to stutter.

I put my fears aside. "That's just Spooky thumping around," I said. I pretended a loud yawn and talked loudly and cheerfully to cover up any more sounds from above. "So," I said, "it's time to get to our rooms. It was fun fooling around with you about all this ghost stuff, Lionel." I gave him a little push in the direction of his room. "Let's go, everyone. Nighty-night."

I gave Claud a meaningful glance that said, Help me here. Good old Claud caught right on. "We had you really going there, didn't we, Lionel?" she said, attempting a laugh.

Lionel looked rather confused. "Yeah," he said. "You win. I'll never play a trick on you again." He walked off towards his room, mumbling something about "hysterical females".

As soon as he'd gone we heard the footsteps again. We ran into Mary Anne's room and closed the door.

"Listen, you lot," I said, "no matter how frightened we are, we have to protect the kids, even Lionel, from what's going on in the mansion."

"But Kristy," Dawn protested, "maybe he's the one who's doing all this stuff. He did try to scare us by pretending to be a ghost."

"But how could he make those noises upstairs?" Claud asked. "He was *with* us."

"Maybe he's got an accomplice," Dawn said.

We talked about that for a while. But in the end we agreed that Lionel probably wasn't responsible for the lights on the third floor. Then, I wondered, who—or what—was?

"Mary Anne," I said, "do you want to sleep in my room tonight?"

"Yes," she said in a quavering voice. "Yes I do." Dawn and Claud said they were going to double up, too.

Mary Anne fell asleep with a pillow over her head. Andrew was sound asleep in his little bed. But I lay wide awake for hours, waiting for more ghostly sounds and thinking about all the scary things that had happened since we'd arrived at the Randolph mansion. I don't know what was more frightening, remembering what had already happened, or worrying about what would happen next.

Claudia

monday
6:00 p.m.

I cant beleve all thats gone on since we came here Saterday night. Thanks for wrighting it all down evrybody. This notebok will be a big help when I rite my compositon for Mrs. Hall. By the way, I'm not worried about having somthing intresting to write about!

"Come on, Claud. Wake up. We need to do some serious detective work today, and this might be the only chance we have to talk privately."

Dawn was leaning over me from the side of her bed. I looked up at her from the nest of blankets I'd made for myself on the floor. "Ghosts," I said sleepily. "I dreamed about ghosts."

"That wasn't a dream," Dawn said. "We heard one again last night. Remember?"

It all came back in a rush. The footsteps above our heads. The blood-curdling scream in the night. Dawn was right. We did have some serious detective work to do. I just hoped I was brave enough to do it.

By the time Jill came knocking on our door to find out what Dawn was going to wear, we had a plan for the day that included sleuthing.

"I'm going to wear a sundress and sandals," Dawn told Jill. Then she added, "Claud and I thought you girls might like to go to the library today. We'll help you sign up for cards and take out some books."

"And I'm going to do some research while we're there," I added, "for an essay I have to write."

Now Karen and Martha were in Dawn's bedroom too. "What are you going to do research on?" Karen asked.

"I'm going to see if I can find out about the history of the Randolph estate," I said. "So

74

let's all get dressed, eat breakfast and go into town."

I decided to wear my floral-print mini-sundress (the pink and red flower pattern is big and sort of abstract). To that I added a pink baseball cap, dangling yellow glass earrings and my red high-top trainers.

After breakfast Dawn and I were ready to take the girls to the library. As we walked around the side of the mansion towards the drive Karen grabbed my hand and tugged at it. "Claudia," she said. "That guy's here again."

I looked around and, sure enough, there was Georgio running across the lawn towards us. There was no way we could avoid him.

"Hi," he said when he reached us. "How's it going?"

"OK," Dawn answered.

Just as he had done the day before, Georgio checked out my clothes. When you dress the way I do you have to expect people to notice. But when Georgio looked at me I felt uncomfortable. Did he think I was *too* wild and colourful?

"We're going to the library," Karen told him. "To take out some books. And Claudia's going to—"

—"choose some books too," I said, completing Karen's sentence. Suddenly, I didn't want Karen to tell Georgio that I was going to research the Randolph mansion. I was suspicious of him, and when you're suspicious of someone, you're careful about what you tell him. (I learned that from all the Nancy Drew mysteries I've read.) To keep the conversation off me, I asked Georgio, "How's it going?"

"Great," Georgio said. "Except I need some advice. I was hoping you could help me."

I didn't even know the guy and he wanted my advice! Advice about what? School? Family problems? Girls? How to menace a houseful of kids?

"Advice about what?" Dawn asked.

"I've noticed that Claudia's got terrific taste in clothes," he said. "And puts colours together in a great way." He was looking me right in the eye. "I'm putting in some new rosebushes and I can't decide which colours to plant where. I wondered if you could help me, Claudia."

"Yeah, OK," I replied. "Why not?"

"I'll go ahead with the kids," Dawn said. "We'll meet you at the library." She flashed me one of those we'll-leave-you-two-alone grins.

When they'd gone, Georgio told me, "The rose garden's on the other side of the house."

Part of me wanted to call out to Dawn, "Wait for me! I'm coming with you lot." But another part of me was happy to follow Georgio. Well, I thought, this is a day devoted to detection and as Georgio's sort of a suspect, I'd better follow him. Besides, I can never resist an artistic challenge.

Twenty-five rosebushes were waiting to be planted. Five each of five shades of red and pink. Georgio told me that Mr Randolph had ordered them from a nursery before he died. "He loved roses," Georgio said. "This will be like a memorial garden for him."

"That's really nice," I replied. I studied the rosebushes for a few minutes, then I asked, "Can we take one rose petal from each bush?"

"Whatever helps," he answered.

When we'd collected the twenty-five rose petals, I sat on a stone bench in the middle of the garden and moved the petals around till I was happy with the arrangement. While I worked with the colours, Georgio dug over the soil.

After about ten minutes I called to him. We looked at the rows of petals I'd arranged on the bench. "This is the layout I would use," I said. "What do you think?"

"I think it's perfect," he replied. "But could you wait till I've got the bushes positioned around the garden before you go? That way I'll be sure to follow your plan exactly."

I walked around the paths of the garden and helped him put the bushes where he'd later plant them. "How are you going to find an outlet for your artistic talent around here?" he asked.

"I'm always doing art projects with the kids I sit for," I told him. I was thinking of the float we were planning for the Founders' Day parade, but decided not to mention it to Georgio.

"You should make a float with the kids for the Founders' Day parade," he said. Could he read my mind?

"Maybe I will," I told him. "Being in a town parade would be a nice way to end our holiday here."

"I thought you were going to be here all summer," he said. He sounded disappointed. But then he added, with that hard-to-read grin of his, "Well, Claudia, let's make the most of the time you have."

What did he mean by that?

"I could help you make that float," he said. "I can build props and you can use my pickup truck."

His pickup truck? I wondered how old you had to be to get a driver's licence in Maine. Was he sixteen plus or eighteen plus? I didn't tell Georgio that if we borrowed his pickup truck for the float we'd have to borrow him to drive it, too.

"Er, I'd better get going," I said. "Babysitting, you know."

"First let me show you a picture of the float some friends and I made last year," he said. "It's in the shed. Come on. It'll only take a minute."

"All the way to the pond?" I said. "It'll take a lot more than a minute."

"You're thinking of the gardener's cottage," he

said. "Where my grandparents used to live. The shed's just around by the garage. That's where I keep my tools."

As we walked to the shed, Georgio told me he used to stay in the gardener's cottage by the pond with his grandparents during the summer. "As no one else is using it," he said, "I still sleep there sometimes."

The shed was small and dark. All my fears about Georgio came flooding back. I wished I hadn't followed him there. I bumped into a big lumpy something and let out a shriek of terror. Was it a dead body?

"What happened?" Georgio asked.

In the half light I made out that the "corpse" was a big bag of sand or something.

"I just bumped into this—stuff," I told Georgio.

"I don't want anything to happen to you," he said. I couldn't tell if he was smiling at me or smirking when he said that. At last he pulled a cord that switched on an overhead lightbulb. We were facing a wall of neatly arranged tools. There were saws, knives, hammers and weapon-like instruments. Georgio reached towards the axe. I was about to make a run for it when his hand landed on a photo that was pinned between the axe and a hammer. He took the photo down and showed it to me. I studied it. Georgio and six other kids were posed in the back of his pickup

79

truck. Their theme was the sixties, so they were dressed like hippies. The pickup truck was painted in psychedelic colours.

"Does your truck still look like that?" I asked.

He laughed. "We used washable paint. Otherwise, I would have been the laughing-stock on campus this year."

I practically choked on the next question. "Are you at college?"

"University of Maine," he said. "Some of these guys on the float were a year ahead of me in high school. And a couple were in tenth grade. I don't make a big deal about age. Some of my friends are a couple of years older than me. Some are a couple of years younger. Like you. You're sixteen, am I right?"

I just nodded. Why didn't I tell him right then that I was thirteen? Maybe I was afraid he'd be angry with me for not having told him sooner. Or maybe I was just keeping to the detective's rule: don't give information to the suspect without a good reason. Or maybe I thought he'd think twice about talking to me so much if he knew how young I was. And the truth was that I wasn't so spooked by him any more. I was kind of enjoying becoming friends with Georgio Trono.

"Anyway," he said. "That was our float."

"It's great," I said. Something else in the shed caught my eye. A candle. An orange candle. A wave of fear coursed through my body. I stepped back from Georgio. Suddenly I wasn't feeling so good about being with him.

"I really have to go," I said. "'Bye."

I burst through the door and into the daylight. Then I ran all the way down the long drive. Lionel had been our "ghost" last night, I knew. Had Georgio been the "ghost" in the corridor the night before that? Just how involved was he?

When I got to the Reese public library my heart was still pounding. I found Dawn in the children's room. She was simultaneously helping Jill choose a book and attempting to stop Karen from introducing Martha to every kid there. This wasn't the time for me to report to Dawn about the incriminating evidence I'd found in the gardener's shed.

I edged Karen away from a crowd of five-year-olds and their day camp counsellor. Somehow I persuaded her that we should go to the cushioned area for some quiet reading time. As we passed Dawn and Jill, Dawn handed me a book. "It's a history of Reese," she said. "The librarian found it for us."

I took the book to the cushioned area and plopped down with Karen and Martha. "*A Historical Tour of Reese*" the title read, "by Millicent Ellsworth." I turned to the index in the back of the book and found two references to the Randolph mansion: Randolph, Mary Sears, p. 108, and Randolph, Reginald, p. 69.

Claudia

On page 69 I read that Reginald Randolph had been a wealthy landholder and fisherman. He had owned a big fleet of fishing boats, and dozens of fishermen had worked for him. He often captained one of the boats himself. On one of those fishing trips, in 1859, Reginald Randolph and a crew of thirteen had been lost at sea.

Turning to page 108 I learned that Reginald's wife, Mary, mourned her husband for the remaining twenty years of her life. From ten o'clock till eleven o'clock every night, Mary, dressed in white, stood on the widow's walk of the mansion and stared out at the sea. The townspeople of that time reported seeing her standing there even in the foulest weather. During a fierce storm in 1879, she was hurled to her death by the winds.

I wrote down names and dates in my notebook. Mary Sears Randolph was an obvious candidate for our third-floor ghost. I couldn't wait to tell the others.

When we got back to the mansion everyone was gathering on the verandah for lunch. The Coopers carried out plates of sandwiches, salad, biscuits and fruit. Lisa suggested that the BSC members might enjoy a break from the kids during lunch. "Thanks," Kristy said.

"That's a great idea," I added.

So the Reese contingent of the BSC took our lunches to a picnic table under a big oak tree. (I was relieved to see that Mrs Menders was making certain that Jill didn't trail after us.)

Before I could tell everybody what I'd learned about Mary Sears Randolph, Mary Anne said, "Claud, I saw you talking to Georgio again. What was all that about?"

I told my friends about helping lay out the rosebushes, and how Georgio had offered to help us with the float for the Founders' Day parade. I even told them about the great sixties float he'd made with his friends.

"I think Georgio's got a crush on you," Kristy put in.

"Listen, you lot," I said. "There's something I haven't told you yet. Actually, there's two things. One is that Georgio's *old*—he's at college and he's got his driving licence."

"That means he could be nineteen, or even older," Dawn exclaimed. "Does he know how old you are, Claud?"

I shook my head no and went right on to the second thing I hadn't told them. "I saw an orange candle in the shed where he keeps his tools. A used one."

"Why would he have a candle in the toolshed?" Kristy asked.

"For light?" Mary Anne suggested. "Maybe there's no electricity in there."

"He turned on a light so I could see the picture

of his sixties float," I told them. "So the shed has got electricity."

"Do you think he's the one who's been trying to scare us?" Dawn asked.

"But we know it was Lionel," Mary Anne said. "We caught him in the act."

"Lionel was carrying a white candle," Dawn pointed out. "The wax we found on the rug was dark orange."

"And we never asked Lionel if he was the one who scared us that first night," I said. "We just assumed he did."

"So, Claud, you're saying we could have two phoney ghosts," Kristy said. "The Lionel ghost last night and the Georgio ghost the night before."

"What about the lights on the third floor?" Mary Anne asked.

"And the footsteps," Kristy added.

"And the scream we heard in the middle of the night," Dawn said.

"There's one more thing I haven't told you lot about Georgio," I said. "He sometimes sleeps in the gardener's cottage."

"You mean he might have been there last night, spying on us," Dawn said with a shudder. "That's creepy."

"Or maybe he wasn't in the cottage," Kristy said, "but on the third floor of the mansion, turning lights off and on."

"But the door's locked," Mary Anne reminded us.

"He's lived on the estate his whole life," I said. "He probably has a way of getting up there. Maybe there's a secret passage."

"So he could have been the one walking up and down the third-floor corridor," Dawn said.

"And screaming in the middle of the night," I added.

"But why would Georgio want to scare us?" Mary Anne asked.

"That's the mystery," I said. "But there's one last thing you don't know." I finished by telling them the tragic story of Reginald Randolph who was lost at sea, and his wife's nightly vigil on the widow's walk.

We looked up at the widow's walk. I imagined Mary Randolph standing there in her white dress . . . every night . . . for twenty years. Even in the midday sun I shivered. I wondered if Mary was now spending her nights haunting the mansion? Or was someone else—Georgio, perhaps—trying to make us *think* the Randolph mansion was haunted?

8th CHAPTER

KAREN

MONDAY

DEAR DADDY,

HI FROM REESE, MAWE. THE HOUSE WE ARE STAYING IN IS A LOT BIGGER THAN THE BIG HOUSE. I AM HELPING THE BABY-SITTERS. MY JOB IS TO MAKE SURE MARTHA MENDERS MAKES FRIENDS IN HER NEW TOWN. IT IS A HARD JOB BECAUSE MARTHA IS SHY. BUT I WILL FIGURE IT OUT. I THINK IT IS LUCKY FOR HER THAT I AM NOT SHY.

YOUR DAUGHTER,
KAREN

P.S.
SEE YOU SOON.

P.P.S.
ANDREW SAYS HI-RIB-BID.

Reese is a small town. But there are lots of kids around. There were loads of them at the beach. And some at the library. I made a promise to myself. By the end of Monday, Martha Menders would have three new friends. And they would all be nice.

After lunch I helped Mary Anne tidy up the porch. "So what are we going to do this afternoon?" I asked her.

"There are some shops I'd like to look at in town," Mary Anne said. "It might be fun to start the afternoon there."

Goody! There would be lots of kids in the kinds of shops they have in Reese. There's one shop called "Fudge Depot" that just sells fudge. And one next to it called "Mity Kites". You can guess what they sell. "I'll go and get Martha," I told Mary Anne.

"I'm going to buy Claudia an early birthday present," Mary Anne said. "So don't invite her, OK?"

"OK," I said.

I love secrets. And I'm *great* at keeping secrets secret. I found Martha swinging in the hammock with Claudia. I told Martha that we were going to town with Mary Anne. Claudia said she might come too. But I told her that Mary Anne had a *special reason* for not wanting her to go shopping with us. Claudia smiled and said, "I'll just rest in the hammock instead of going with you, then."

"I'm going to stay here, too," Martha said. "I want to read *The Secret Garden*." That was the book she'd taken out of the library.

I put on a pout and told Martha that I love shopping and I wanted to look for presents for my family. And that I needed her help. The pouting worked because Martha climbed out of the comfy hammock and came with me.

On the way to town Mary Anne asked Martha how she liked Reese so far. Martha said, "I want to go back to Boston. We live in a big flat in a new building with a lift. That's where my best friend Louise lives."

I thought I was Martha's best friend. At least while I was visiting her. Well, I would be her best friend soon. Just wait till I introduced her to lots of kids in Reese. I knew that Martha and I and all her new friends would have loads of fun together. I'm like Kristy. I enjoy challenges.

"Here we are," Mary Anne said. "This is the shop where I'm sure I'll find a good present for Claudia." It was an art supplies shop.

We went inside. Mary Anne and Martha walked up and down the aisles looking for the perfect present for Claudia. I walked up and down the aisles looking for the perfect friend for Martha. All I could find were teenagers or kids who were a lot younger than us. Bother!

My luck changed when Mary Anne was standing at the cash register buying a face-painting set for Claudia. Martha was sticking to Mary Anne like glue. And I was looking at a packet of construction paper and thinking about what I could make with it.

Here's the good luck part. A girl of my age (and Martha's) walked into the shop with her mother. The girl looked familiar to me. Then I remembered why. I ran to her and said, "Hi. I saw you on the beach yesterday. You had on a red two-piece swimsuit with butterflies."

"Oh," was all the girl replied. Then she looked at the floor. Her mother said, "We were at the beach yesterday, but I don't remember Amber playing with you."

"We didn't *officially* meet," I admitted. "But I noticed her. And I thought, that girl would like to meet my friend Martha. Martha Menders who's just moved to Reese. Martha's loads of fun. So here she is—Martha Menders!" I turned to the cash register where Mary Anne and Martha had been standing. They had gone.

"I think your friends have left," Amber's mother said.

I looked through the shop window and saw that she was right. Martha and Mary Anne were already waiting outside for me. Martha was holding Mary Anne's hand and looking down at the pavement. But Mary Anne was looking at me. She signalled for me to come out.

I signalled for her to come back into the shop. She shook her head no.

"I have to go now," I told Amber and her mother. "But don't forget," I added with a big smile. "Martha Menders. She's really nice."

When I ran outside I told Mary Anne, "You shouldn't have kept telling me to come out. You should have come back inside. I met a perfect friend for Martha. Her name's Amber and she's shy too."

"Karen, I think you should let Martha meet people in her own way," Mary Anne said.

I didn't think Mary Anne Spier was the best person to give me advice about how to help Martha meet people. After all, next to Martha, Mary Anne's the shyest person I know.

Now my stepsister, Kristy, isn't shy. That's one of the things I love about her. And Kristy knows how to take action and make things happen. So I was glad when we saw Kristy walking towards us on Main Street. (Jason and Andrew were with her.)

"Where are you lot going?" I asked.

Kristy was carrying her baseball glove and a bat. She was wearing a baseball cap. Jason had a glove too, and his new softball.

"Come on," he said to Kristy. "Let's go."

"Just a sec," she replied. Then she told us she was taking Jason to the recreation ground to meet some boys of his own age. The recreation ground!

It was just like Kristy to come up with an idea like that. A recreation ground was the perfect place to meet kids.

"Girls!" Jason mumbled. "Everywhere we go there are more girls." Jason can be really silly sometimes.

"Why don't we take Andrew with us?" Mary Anne suggested. "We're looking at some of the shops we missed yesterday. Then we're going to look at the boats in the harbour."

"That'd be great," Kristy told Mary Anne. "Jason and I will catch up with you later. Let's go, Jason."

But Jason was already walking down the street.

"Wait for me, Jason," Kristy called as she ran after him.

"Let's go, kids," Mary Anne said to us.

"We're going to the recreation ground too," I said. I grabbed Martha's hand and yanked her down the street. When we caught up with Kristy she called back to Mary Anne that she would babysit for us, and Mary Anne could just take Andrew to the harbour. I wanted to see the boats in the harbour too. But I knew it was more important to help Martha make friends.

At the recreation ground was a ball field, a playground and a big barn. Several boys of Jason's age were playing softball. And some kids were playing on the slides and the jungle gym. "Jason and I are going to the ballfield," Kristy said. "You girls stay here." She whispered to me, "Jason wants to meet boys of his own age. I need you to stay out of the way for a while. OK?"

Martha and I played on the swings, but I kept an eye on how Jason was doing. Kristy was throwing the softball to him. He could catch and hit a softball pretty well. I'm on Kristy's softball team so I know a lot about softball. The boys playing in the field weren't so good. I couldn't understand why they didn't ask Jason to play. And Kristy too. She could have helped them have more fun. At home we have much more fun when Kristy plays softball with us than when we try to play games on our own. Maybe Martha could play softball, I thought. Maybe if we started playing with Kristy those other boys would invite us to play with them. And I knew some of those boys must have younger sisters for Martha to meet.

Martha and I were swinging to and fro on the baby swings, pushing sand with our feet. "Martha," I said, "come on. Kristy wants us on the ballfield."

"No, she doesn't," Martha said. "I've been watching."

"She does," I said. "I know what Kristy's thinking and she wants to teach you softball. She's my sister and I can read her mind."

"No, you can't," Martha said.

"I can. I know she wants us to come over right now and you have to do it because she's our babysitter."

"No, I don't," Martha said.

I lost my temper. I couldn't help it. "You have to because I said so," I yelled. "I need to find some friends for you so you'll like living here. Help a little. Say hello to the people I introduce you to. Look them in the eye. Why do you have to be so shy?" I was so angry I kicked some sand in her direction.

She kicked more sand back at me. "Why do you have to annoy me?" she asked.

"Because I like you," I shouted. I kicked sand at her again. But the wind blew it back in my face.

"I'm sorry," Martha said.

I thought it was so funny that I'd kicked the sand but she'd apologized that I had to giggle. "You didn't kick it," I told her. "I did."

"But I kicked sand too," Martha said. "So I'm sorry."

"Me too," I said. "I'm sorry I shouted."

"Are we still friends?" Martha asked.

"Of course we are."

Martha had a lot to learn about friendship. You can be friends even if you have a fight.

"Come on," I said. "We can help Kristy play ball with Jason."

Martha followed me to the softball field. Jason looked a bit disappointed to see us. Kristy did

93

too. But sometimes you have to ignore what people think and do what you know is right for your friends. Those other boys were stupid. They didn't ask any of us to play ball with them. Even when they saw me play. Which shows you how much they know about softball. Not much.

LOGAN

WEDNESDAY

DEAR MARY ANNE,
  I MISS YOU. A LOT.
  I'M NOT THE ONLY ONE WHO MISSES
YOU! WAIT UNTIL I TELL YOU WHAT
HAPPENED AT THE BSC MEETING TODAY.
FOR ME IT ALL STARTED AFTER THE
MEETING, WHEN MALLORY CAME LOOKING
FOR ME AT THE ROSEBUD CAFE . . .

The Rosebud Cafe, where I'm working as a waiter, is usually pretty busy. That's why our boss says, "No phone calls or friends dropping in while you're working." I made sure to tell this to my friends when I started the job. So I was pretty surprised when a so-called friend of mine— Mallory Pike—burst into the Rosebud on Monday and started trailing me while I cleared tables and served water and bread. And she was talking a mile a minute!

"Mal, I can't talk now," I hissed at her over my shoulder. "Can't you see I'm busy?"

"You don't understand, Logan," she insisted. "This is important."

"You can't follow me around, Mal," I insisted. "My boss will have a fit. I'll get fired."

"OK. I'll stay right here." Mallory stood between the counter, where I pick up water and bread, and the door to the kitchen, where I take trays of dirty plates. As I made trips up and down, Mal told me what had happened at the Monday BSC meeting.

I wasn't at the meeting (obviously) and neither was Shannon. It was just Mal and Jessi in Claudia's room. Mal had been acting chairman and Jessi had been acting secretary.

The first thing Mal and Jessi did was check the answering machine. But there were no messages.

"Do you think that's because people know that Kristy and the others aren't here?" Jessi asked,

"Maybe Jake told all the other kids that they'd get *us* if they rang for sitters."

"I don't know," Mal answered. "Maybe."

"How did things go with the twins at the Prezziosos'?"

"I barely survived," Mal told her. "It's the sort of job that would be better with two sitters. I've already written about it in the notebook." She sighed. "But I'm babysitting for them again tomorrow—solo."

Just then the phone rang. Mal looked at the clock and saw that it was exactly five-thirty. The call was from Mrs Arnold, asking for me (Logan) to get to my job (the one I hadn't heard about yet) at her place a few minutes early.

Mal was afraid Mrs Arnold could hear her voice shaking when she told her, "Of course, Mrs Arnold. I'll get in touch with Logan straight away. He'll be there by seven-fifteen at the latest." When she rang off, Mal asked Jessi, "Did you tell Logan about that job at the Arnolds' tonight?"

"I thought you were going to," Jessi answered.

"I forgot," Mal confessed. "We'd better call him straight away."

Jessi checked the schedule I'd given them and saw that I was working at the Rosebud until six-thirty. "Even though he told us not to, I'm going to phone him at the restaurant," Mal said. "It's an emergency."

But before she could pick up the phone, it rang again. This time it was Mal's mother needing a sitter for the next day. Mal told her there were no sitters available. "But I'm one of your oldest and best clients," Mrs Pike complained, only half-joking. Mallory felt awful about disappointing her mother. But what could she do?

The phone rang again. This time it was a new client who'd heard about the BSC from the Braddocks. "I'm sorry," Mal said, "but we haven't got any sitters available tomorrow afternoon. Please call us again."

"Don't forget to phone Logan," Jessi reminded Mal. Before Mal could make the call there was a knock on Claud's door. "It's me. Janine." Claudia's sister poked her head round the door.

"We're having a Babysitters Club meeting," Jessi told her.

"I need to speak to you," Janine replied.

"When our meeting's over," Mal said. "We've got a lot of calls to make."

"More than you think," Janine said.

"What do you mean?" Mal asked.

"First of all, did you know that your answering machine isn't on?"

Mal and Jessi checked the machine and saw that she was right.

"So that's why we didn't have any calls," Jessi said.

98

"On the contrary," Janine said. "You had several calls. On our family phone line. When your answering machine didn't take calls, your clients called us. Here."

She handed Mal six messages. One of them was from Shannon, listing the times when she could babysit. It was a short list. All the others were from clients requesting sitters. Just then the phone rang with another client needing a sitter. Mal said she'd call right back.

"Janine," Mal said when she rang off, "er, how would you like to make some extra money?"

Janine agreed to take one job. "I certainly don't want to see the club destroyed because some of its members are on an out-of-town assignment," she said.

The club destroyed? Janine had just put Jessi and Mal's worst nightmare into words.

"So," Janine continued, "I'll take one night job. But I can't oblige you tonight." She grinned. "Because I've got a date."

They gave Janine a job with the Hobarts for the following night.

When she'd left, the meeting lasted an extra twenty minutes, while Mal and Jessi returned clients' calls. Out of six jobs, they had to turn down four. At that point, Mal told me, they were so desperate for more babysitters that they considered calling Stacey McGill, our ex-treasurer, to see if she'd help out.

"We can't ask Stacey to help us," Jessi said. "Even if she said she'd take a job, she might not turn up for it. You know she puts Robert before anything else."

"That's what's so great about Mary Anne and Logan," Mal said.

"*Logan!*" they screamed in unison as they remembered that they still hadn't told me about my job with the Arnolds.

"Mal," Jessi said with a gasp, "phone him. Quick!"

Mal tried calling the Rosebud, but kept getting an engaged signal. How could she know that my boss takes the phone off the hook when things are really busy? And believe me, that afternoon we were really busy.

"I'd better go over there," Mal said. "It's already six-twenty-five."

"Six-twenty-five?" Jessi said. "Oh no! I told Becca I'd teach her how to Rollerblade at six o'clock. Dinner's at six-thirty and then I'm sitting for Becca and Squirt. My parents and Aunt Cecelia are going to that auction for the Ambulance Squad."

"If there *is* an auction," Mal cried. "I'd better find Logan fast."

Mal and Jessi had already dashed down the stairs when Jessi remembered the answering machine and ran back to turn it on. By then Mal was jogging towards the Rosebud Cafe.

100

"But I can't sit tonight, Mal," I said, when she'd finished her tale of woe. I was filling water glasses. "When this shift is over, I'm going on to the night shift. As a favour for a friend."

"How could you?" Mal practically shouted. "Tonight's the night you said you could babysit."

"When you two didn't call with a job, I thought I was free." (Now I was slicing French bread.) "So I told this guy, Carlos, I'd take his shift. You'll have to find someone else to sit."

"There's no one else!" Mal shrieked. She was getting so panicky her face was as red as her hair, and she was moving around like a Mexican jumping bean.

"Mal, quieten down," I said. I picked up another loaf of bread to slice. "Get a grip on yourself."

She grabbed the bread from my hand and shook it violently. "You get a grip," she said between clenched teeth. The loaf of bread collpsed like a rag doll. She carried on shaking it at me anyway. "This is important," she hissed. "Mrs Arnold is running the auction for the ambulance squad. If people die because there's no ambulance, it'll be your fault."

My boss, who was showing customers to a table, looked over to see what the disturbance was about. The other waiter (or rather waitress) on the Monday afternoon shift was Geraldine Breslin. She stood in front of Mal so that our boss

101

LOGAN

wouldn't see that Mal was mangling his French bread.

When at last Mal stopped to catch her breath, Geraldine whispered, "What's going on here?"

I asked Geraldine if she could do me the enormous favour of taking the shift I'd said I would take for Carlos.

"Please, oh please, please," Mal begged Geraldine. By then Mal was wringing the bread like a handkerchief.

"I suppose I'd better," Geraldine said, "before all we have left to serve the customers are breadcrumbs."

MAL — ACTING PRESIDENT OF THE BABY-SITTERS CLUB — WAS STILL HOLDING ON TO THAT PATHETIC LOAF OF BREAD WHEN I RUSHED HER OUT OF THE RESTAURANT.

"OH, THANK YOU, THANK YOU, LOGAN," SHE EXCLAIMED. "YOU'RE A WONDERFUL GUY. NO WONDER MARY ANNE LOVES YOU. I LOVE YOU. WE ALL LOVE YOU. STONEYBROOK AMBULANCE SERVICES SHOULD NAME AN AMBULANCE AFTER YOU."

AT THAT MOMENT I WASN'T FEELING VERY LOVING TOWARD MAL. BUT I LOVE YOU, MARY ANNE — EVEN IF YOU DO HAVE SOME GOOFY FRIENDS. I CAN'T WAIT UNTIL YOU COME HOME.

LOVE, LOGAN

Dawn

Monday
11 p.m.

Kristy, I know that helping
the Menders kids adjust to
the idea of living in Reese is
more important than solving
mysteries. But I'm beginning
to think they shouldn't live
in a haunted house. And
this house is definitely,
positively haunted. Yes, some
of the noises we hear at
night are just the creaks of
a big old house. But the
footsteps I heard over my
head a few minutes ago
are <u>footsteps</u>. They couldn't

be anything else. And I also heard an eerie sound in the wall of my bedroom. It sounded like a cry for help. Was it Mary's ghost? Or another ghost?

"But I don't *want* to meet any other kids," Jill protested. "And I don't want to play with Karen and Martha. They're too young. I want to play— I mean hang around—with you, Dawn."

It was Monday afternoon. Kristy, Jason and Andrew were at the playground. Mary Anne had taken Martha and Karen shopping. That left Claudia, Jill and me, swinging in the hammock under the pine trees. Jill and I were watching Claud sketch the mansion, which was mostly a drawing of the widow's walk. I was *desperate* to talk to Claudia about Mary Randolph and Georgio Trono. But Jill was glued to me, as usual. And she had no intention of "playing" with anyone else.

"Where's Spooky?" I asked Jill. "Why don't you play with your cat?"

"Spooky's disappeared," she said.

"When did you last see him?" Claudia asked.

"Last night. Before I went to bed. He was in the hall and I said, "'Come on, Spooky, you can sleep in here.' But he ran away from me."

Dawn

Claudia and I exchanged a look behind Jill's back. We both thought that Spooky was . . . spooky.

"So what have you planned for my entertainment this afternoon?" a booming voice asked. Lionel had sneaked up on us. Again.

I jumped so high I almost fell out of the hammock. "Lionel!" I shouted. "Stop sneaking up on us."

"You scare easily," he said. He sat on the ground near us and gave the hammock little pushes.

"So," he said, "what's the plan? Or are the babysitters just going to sit around all day?"

"You know what might be fun?" Claudia asked. "We could eat in the dining room tonight. And dress up for dinner."

"Wow! Great! I mean, if you think so, Dawn," said Jill.

"I think that would be great fun," I replied.

"We'll lay the table with all the best china and silverware that's in the dining room cabinet," Claud continued. "It's probably been in your family for a zillion years, Lionel."

"Some of Uncle Edward's suits are sixty or seventy years old. I saw them in the wardrobe," Lionel said. "Perhaps I'll wear his dinner jacket."

Yes! At last we'd finally hit on an idea that Lionel liked.

Dawn

I wished there were some old-fashioned women's clothes around, too. We'd have to put together outfits from the clothes we'd brought. I knew Claud would help us organize that part. But first we had to get permission from Lionel's parents, and talk to the Coopers.

Mr and Mrs Menders thought having a formal dinner was a terrific idea and said they'd be back from their afternoon of research in plenty of time to "dress for dinner".

Claud, Lionel, Jill and I went to the kitchen to talk to the Coopers. Elton said they'd be glad to make a special dinner. They'd been hoping for an opportunity to use the good china. Margaret beamed her big smile and rubbed her hands together as if she couldn't wait to start cooking something special.

"You lay the table and we'll see to the cooking," Elton told us.

"And, of course, we'll help clear up after dinner," Claud said.

In the dining room we put out the best dishes, silverware and crystal that we'd seen in the cabinet. Lionel opened the french doors to the verandah to air the room, and we set to work. I read the directions on the silver polish bottle and showed Jill what to do. Claud and Lionel went to the kitchen to wash and dry the crystal glasses.

"Everyone gets two glasses," Claud said

when she came back with a tray of sparkling glasses.

"Two forks and three spoons," I added.

Mrs Cooper brought us a linen tablecloth and napkins. At last we were ready to lay the table. On the dishes was a delicate, hand-painted rose pattern.

"Some of the roses that Georgio planted look just like these," Claud said. (She looked quite dreamy when she said that.) Then she had a very Claud idea. "Let's make placecards," she said. "I can copy the rose pattern from the dishes."

That's when Lionel announced that he'd had his fill of our afternoon project and went off to his room.

When we'd finished laying the table I stepped back to take a look. "You know what we're missing?" I said. "A candelabra."

"There's one," Jill said. She was pointing to the top shelf in the cabinet. I found a stool in the kitchen and climbed up to look at the candelabra.

As I took it down I could see that it needed a good cleaning. It wasn't dusty, but whoever used it last hadn't cleaned off the wax drippings.

I handed it to Claudia before I stepped off the stool. "That's interesting," Claud said. "The wax on here is orange."

"Why is that interesting?" Jill asked.

I gave Claud a Look over Jill's head. "Because

people don't use orange candles that much," I said.

"I saw some pink candles in a drawer in the cabinet," Claud said. "We'll use those."

While I cleaned and polished the candelabra, Jill and Claud made placecards.

"Wouldn't it be great if we could have some of the roses from the garden for the table?" Claud said.

The moment she said that, Georgio walked through the french doors. He was carrying the most beautiful bouquet of roses I'd ever seen. "I thought you might like these for your dinner party," he said as he handed them to Claudia. "There's one rose from each of the bushes I planted this morning."

I could tell Claudia was rattled. I was, too. First of all, the instant Claudia said she wanted roses, Georgio appeared with them. Secondly, he knew we were having a dinner party and we hadn't told him. Maybe Elton had told him, but still it *felt* weird.

Georgio admired the way we'd laid the table. "If you need candles," he said, "I've got some in the shed. They're orange, though. Maybe they wouldn't go."

"We don't want orange candles," Jill said. "We're using pink."

"Whatever Claudia thinks will look best, will definitely look best," Georgio said. "She's got great taste." Then he left the way he'd come. Through the french doors.

Hmmm. If Georgio was our "ghost" the first night, he certainly wasn't trying to keep his orange candles a secret.

By the way, I was right about Claud helping us with clothes. She had brought *two* long skirts. So I wore one with my pink tank top and Claud's long rope of fake pearls. Jill wore a skirt of mine, which was long on her. ("I want to dress just like you, Dawn.") I did my hair—and Jill's—in French plaits. Kristy and Mary Anne, who might not ordinarily be too excited about dressing for dinner, got into the mood when they saw all the work we'd done in the dining room.

"It's so elegant!" Mary Anne said.

"This is great," Kristy added.

"Oh goody, goody, triple goody!" Karen exclaimed. "We can be Lovely Ladies! Come on, Martha. We have to look through my mother's clothes. And your mother's. And we can wear make-up and jewellery and high heels." She grabbed Martha's hand, and they ran out of the room.

"Uh-oh!" Kristy said as she went out after them.

By seven o'clock we were sipping fizzy punch "cocktails" in the parlour. Lionel and Claudia were helping the Coopers in the kitchen and dining room with last-minute details. A bell rang.

The doors between the parlour and dining room opened, and Lionel and Claud appeared, Lionel looking really smart in his great-uncle's dinner jacket, Claud looking amazing in a full-length black gauze skirt over a black leotard. She was wearing dangling glass earrings that she'd made from an old chandelier. Her long black hair was held back on one side with a single red rose.

Lionel bowed like a butler. "Ladies and gentlemen," he announced, "dinner is served."

The dinner was delicious. We started with an appetizer of bite-sized pizzas. Then we had a green salad followed by a main course of roast chicken and mashed potatoes. While we were eating our elegant dessert (ice cream with caramel sauce and wafer-thin cookies), Mr Menders tapped his glass. "I'd like to propose a toast," he said.

We lifted our glasses. "First, I want to thank you all for this lovely party. Second, I want to say that our plan to set up a business here is coming along well. We have a lot more research to do, but things are looking good. We may very well be able to move to Reese permanently."

"DAD!" Lionel shouted (in his *own* voice). "How can you say that, when you promised us we'd have a say in the decision? That it was our decision too? Reese is the most boring place in the world! I won't be able to pursue my acting career here. I for one *do not want to move to Reese*."

111

"I don't like it either," Jason said. "The kids are stuck-up."

Mr and Mrs Menders looked disappointed. "What about you, Martha?" Mrs Menders asked.

"I want to go back to Boston." Martha had to say it twice before her mother could hear her. But I heard it the first time.

"And I want to move to Stoneybrook in the house right next to Dawn's," said Jill.

Kristy, Claud, Mary Anne and I looked helplessly at one another. We were supposed to be helping the kids adjust. So far we hadn't done a very good job.

That night the parents said they'd put their own kids to bed while my friends and I helped in the kitchen. There were a lot of dishes to do, and we had to be extremely careful because everything was antique, and some of it was fragile.

While Kristy and Mary Anne cleared the table, Claud and I washed the dishes from the first course and Mr and Mrs Cooper put away their cooking utensils and generally cleared up.

"So," Mr Cooper said, "are you girls still thinking about the lights you saw on the third floor?"

"Yes," Claud admitted. "But there's something else."

She told the Coopers what we had learned about Reginald and Mary Randolph at the

112

library. Then she asked, "Was that the story you didn't want to tell us last night?"

"No," Elton said. "Though of course, I knew about Mary Randolph's terrible grief and tragic end. I was thinking of—"

Mrs Cooper banged her hand on the table and shook her head no. Mr Cooper said, "Now Margaret, these girls are mature enough to handle a little history. They're interested in the mansion, and Lydia is part of the story."

"Who's Lydia?" I asked.

By then Mary Anne and Kristy had come back with trays of dirty dishes. So all four of us were there when Elton told us about Lydia Randolph.

"Lydia Randolph was the granddaughter of Reginald and Mary Randolph," he began. "I've heard that Lydia was a beautiful dark-haired young woman who was having a romance with the gardener's son. He was a handsome young man called George, who worked on the estate as a groom in the stables. Lydia's paternal grandparents were dead by then. It was her parents who found out about the romance and forbade her to see George again. To that end, they fired both George and his father and forced the entire family to leave the estate. But George returned secretly. Lydia's parents found her with him in the gardener's cottage.

"Her parents locked Lydia in one of the back bedrooms on the third floor. She was a prisoner in her own home. The seasons passed. Then a year passed. And another. And another. Until five years had passed and that poor girl was still imprisoned.

"During those years George had made a career for himself and a small fortune. It was all done so that he might convince the Randolphs that he was worthy of their daughter. But when George came back to Reese as a successful businessman, the Randolphs wouldn't receive him and repeatedly ordered him to be turned away. Where, George wondered, was Lydia? Had she married someone else? Had she died? At last a servant told George that his beloved was imprisoned on the third floor.

"George couldn't rest till he found a way to free Lydia. At last he managed to make his way to the third floor. Some say he built a secret passage, but I've never seen one. Anyway, he did get up there. But he couldn't find Lydia. There was only one person on the third floor, a white-haired old woman living in one of the back rooms.

"'Where's my Lydia?' he asked the old woman."

"'*I* am Lydia,' she answered."

I gasped. So did Claud. Mary Anne turned so pale I was afraid she'd faint.

"Tragic," Elton said. "Terribly tragic."

"What happened next?" I asked him in a whisper.

"I don't know. But strange things happened on these old estates. So don't let it scare you."

"But this happened here," Claud murmured fearfully.

"Well, that's all very interesting," Kristy told Elton. Then she said to us, "Let's finish up in here. I'm calling an emergency BSC meeting. As Andrew's sleeping in my room we'll meet in Mary Anne's room in half an hour."

I couldn't wait to be alone with my friends to talk about Lydia Randolph. Which is exactly what Claudia and I were doing when we walked into Mary Anne's room for the meeting thirty minutes later.

I sat on the bed next to Mary Anne. "It was so creepy," I said with a shudder.

Kristy came in right behind me and announced, "I call this emergency meeting of the Babysitters Club to order."

When everyone was quiet I said, "Listen, you lot, did you notice that Lydia's boyfriend's name was *George* and he was the *gardener's* son? And her name was Lydia, which sounds a lot like Claudia."

"It's all too weird," Claudia said.

But Kristy didn't want to hear anything about mysteries or ghosts. "I repeat," she said sternly, "I call this emergency meeting of the Babysitters Club to order."

115

Dawn

"Isn't the meeting about what Elton's just told us?" I asked.

"It certainly is not," Kristy answered. "We're having this meeting to talk about the kids. We're not doing a very good job. It's our responsibility to help the kids adjust, and they're obviously not adjusting. Did you hear what they said at dinner? None of them is happy here. Not one of them."

Kristy was right. So for the rest of the meeting we talked about the kids. My main concern was how to persuade Jill to spend time with someone besides me. "If only she'd play with Martha," I said. "I must find something that they both love doing and make them do it together."

Claudia had an idea about how we might help Lionel. "Wednesday's our night off," she said. "Let's invite Lionel to go out for a pizza with us, and then we'll go to the summer stock play. It'll be our treat."

"And while we're at the play, we'll make sure he meets some of the people who work there," I added. "Especially kids of his age."

"You mean we're going to see *Dracula*?" Mary Anne asked. "I don't know." She shivered.

But we all knew it was the best thing we could do for Lionel. And what was best for the Menders kids had to be our main concern.

At the end of the meeting we went back to our rooms. As Claud hadn't slept very well on my floor the night before, she decided to sleep in her

116

own room that night. If we were going to be first-rate sitters the next day, we needed our sleep.

Even when I heard the footsteps above me, I stayed in my room. And when I heard that eerie cry in the wall, I stayed in my room too. I was so terrified, so petrified, that I probably couldn't have moved if I'd wanted to.

I tried writing in the BSC Reese notebook for a while. But I couldn't write about the kids. All I could think about was ghosts. At last I worked up the nerve to turn off the light. I lay there, staring into the dark.

Then my heart stopped. Absolutely stopped. I heard the very last thing I wanted to hear: the sound of my door creaking open. I reached for the light, but before I could find the switch, something landed on my legs. I screamed. I turned on the light. It was Spooky. The cat sat on my stomach and stared into my eyes. I could hardly breathe. When I looked away from him I saw a white-robed figure standing in my doorway. Who—or what—was coming towards me? I tried to scream again but, just the way it happens in nightmares, no sound came out.

That was when I realized it was Jill walking into my room. She was wearing a long white nightie. Phew! Spooky jumped off the bed and bounded out of the room. I drew a deep, shaky breath.

117

Dawn

"I found Spooky under my bed, Dawn," Jill said. "I wanted to tell you. But he jumped out of my arms and you scared him away again."

I scared *him*?

At last I found my voice. "Sh-sh!" I told Jill. "We'll wake the others." I climbed out of bed. "Come on. I'll take you back to your room."

I turned on all the lights in my room and the one in the hall. And I made sure to close my door behind me. I didn't want anyone—or any*thing*—coming in while I was out.

118

11th CHAPTER

Mary Anne

Tuesday
2:00 p.m.

I loved going through all the old things in the attic this morning. Sometimes I daydream about how it would have been to live in a town like Reese a hundred years ago. Actually, it's hard to think of anything but ghosts right now, but I'm trying. Really, there has to be some logical explanation for everything that's happening here.

119

"There go our outdoor plans for the kids," Kristy said.

We were in her room helping Andrew get dressed for the day. A rainy day.

"Boats," Andrew said. "Kristy and I want to go and see the boats again."

Kristy handed Andrew a pair of clean socks. "Today you can draw pictures of boats," she told him.

Dawn, Claudia and Jill burst into the room then.

"I know the perfect rainy-day activity," Claudia announced. "We can explore the attic."

"That's a great idea!" I exclaimed. "I bet there's a lot of stuff up there."

"And we can make an inventory for the Menderses," Kristy suggested. "The contents of the attic are part of their inheritance."

"What about what Georgio said?" I asked.

"He was just trying to scare us," Claud said. "Don't worry about it."

"I bet there'll be some wonderful old things up there," I said.

"Like old photo albums," Dawn said.

"And antique clothes," Claud added. "We might find some ideas and costumes for our float."

At breakfast Seth and Lisa and the Menderses told us that their plan for the day was to visit the business area in Reese and a couple of nearby

120

towns to make a study of how many people shopped on a rainy summer's day. When we told them *our* plan, they agreed that it was a perfect rainy-day activity.

"There's just one problem," Claudia said. "The door to the staircase that leads to the third floor is locked."

"I know," Mr Menders said. He told us that he'd been up on the top floor once, when he surveyed the house after the reading of his uncle's will. "But after that," he said, "the key disappeared."

"And the Coopers' set of keys doesn't have one either," Mrs Menders added.

Mr Menders handed Claud his set of keys. "Give my keys one more try," he said. "If none of them works for you either, ask Elton to break the lock. We'll have to go up there sooner or later."

"What's the third floor like?" Dawn asked.

"Well, as you know," Mr Menders answered, "the stairs began in your second-floor corridor. At the top of the stairs to the right is a door to the attic. To the left is a corridor with bedrooms off it. I only went into a couple of them. It's pretty obvious that they haven't been used in generations."

While the rest of the sitters and kids searched through old bureau drawers and cabinets for the missing key, Claud and I ran upstairs and tried all the keys on Mr Menders's keyring. He was right. None of them worked.

By then Kristy, Dawn and the kids had brought us the handful of keys they'd found around the house. While Claud tried those, I went back to my room to find a pad and pen for making a list of the contents of the attic. When I looked out of my window to see if the rain was slowing down, I noticed Georgio working in one of the gardens. I thought it was strange for him to be working outside in a heavy downpour. I thought it was even stranger that he wasn't paying much attention to his work. He kept glancing up at the mansion, as if he were looking for something—or someone. I backed away from the window. I didn't want him to see me. I had a feeling that Georgio was spying on us.

I found a notebook and a pen and went back to the locked door where Kristy was saying, "I'll go and ask Mr Cooper to break the lock."

"Can I help you with something?" a male voice asked.

Claud jumped about a mile, and I yelped.

It was Georgio. He seemed to have appeared out of nowhere.

"Sorry I scared you," he said. "I just wondered if I could help."

What was he doing in the house? How did he know we needed help?

"We're going to explore the attic," Karen said. "But we can't get in."

"I really don't think you should go up there," Georgio replied.

"Mr and Mrs Menders told us we could," Claud said.

"My dad's lost the key," Jill added.

"Have *you* got a key?" Karen asked.

Georgio hesitated for a second. Then he said quietly, "I might have."

"Then try to open the door for us," Kristy said. "Please."

Georgio took a set of keys from his belt. He selected a key and unlocked the door easily with it.

"Oh, goody!" Karen said. "You're our hero."

I didn't think Georgio was a hero. I was just about convinced he was our third-floor "ghost".

Before he left us Georgio said, "Be careful. If you need me for anything I'll be in the garden. You can call me from the window."

As we climbed the stairs I felt as afraid of Georgio as I did of the attic. But after the first few minutes up there I was so interested and busy that for a while I forgot about being afraid.

The attic was everything we had hoped it would be—and more. I was so busy writing down what everyone else was finding, that at first I didn't make any discoveries myself. But I did see a lot of wonderful antiques.

Mary Anne

Here are just some of the things we found:

sewing form (woman)
sewing form (man)
antique baby carriage
2 sleds
trunk of baby clothes
hundreds of old magazines
two photo albums
trunk of children's toys
2 rocking chairs
croquet set
large armoire (clothes closet)

While Kristy and Jason pawed through the trunk of toys with the younger children, the rest of us continued the survey of the attic.

I tested the handle of the armoire. "It isn't locked," I told Dawn. "But I'm afraid to open it. There might be bats in there." I backed away while Lionel pulled the doors open. Of course he had to say something about bats and Dracula while he did it. "Don't you know, my dear, that we sleep in our coffins during the day? Not in some dusty old cupboard."

There were no bats in the armoire. It wasn't dusty either. It held three white cotton garment bags. Two were snapped closed, but the middle one was open. We looked inside the open bag first. It held two gowns. One was yellow satin with a smocked bodice. The other was dark blue velvet with black lace trim. I inspected the smocking and handmade lace. "The handiwork on these is amazing," I told the others. "It's so intricate." (I love to do what Claud calls "the sewing arts". I've learned how to embroider, smock and make quilts.)

Claud and Dawn opened the other two garment bags. All the gowns were distinctive and beautiful.

"Oh, I wish we'd found these before our formal dinner!" exclaimed Claudia.

"Why are there three gowns in each of these bags," Dawn wondered out loud, "but only two in the middle one?"

"Maybe there were only eight gowns to put away," I said.

"Then why wasn't the bag closed?" Dawn asked. "Whoever put these gowns away was very careful with the others."

Claud looked around to be sure the kids couldn't hear her when she asked, "Do you think these were Lydia's gowns?"

But Lionel heard her. "Lydia," he intoned. "Oh, my beloved Lydia. They can't separate us. I will rescue you. A team of wild horses couldn't keep me away from you."

When he'd finished his performance, Dawn asked him, "How'd you know about Lydia?"

125

"Elton told me. I assume that's who told you."

"He told me, too," Jill piped up.

I was surprised that Mr Cooper had told Jill the story of Lydia. I thought that was a pretty scary story to tell a kid.

"It's probably not true," I said. "Sometimes people make up a story, like at Halloween, and the people who hear it think it's true."

"I don't care," Jill said. "Dawn and I don't scare easily. Do we, Dawn?"

Dawn just sighed.

While Dawn and Claudia snapped the garment bags closed, I peered into the toy box. I wanted to include some of the larger toys on my list. "What did you lot find?" I asked.

"Things you'd love," Kristy responded. "They're ancient."

"We have to be very careful with these toys," Karen said, holding up an antique porcelain doll, "because they might be worth a lot of money."

Andrew showed me a faded red wooden boat about the size of a loaf of bread. "This is my boat," he said. "I like boats."

Kristy explained to Andrew that he could play with the boat while we were in the attic, but that it wasn't his, and it would have to go back into the trunk.

The next big discovery of the morning was two photo albums in the drawer of the armoire. Claud opened one book to a black and white photo of a

126

beautiful young woman. "I bet this is Lydia," she said. I recognized the woman's dress. It was the satin gown with the smocked bodice. Looking at that picture gave me chills.

The photo albums were fascinating. I loved seeing the way people dressed, and how Reese looked so long ago.

"This man looks so much like somebody I know," Claud said. She was pointing to a photo of a middle-aged man. He had on one of those stiff pointy collars men used to wear in the early nineteen hundreds.

"Someone in Stoneybrook?" I asked.

"Maybe," Claud answered. "I wish I could work out who." She turned the page. "It'll come to me later."

"I'm sick of being up here," I heard Jason complain to Kristy. "All we're doing is looking at old toys and *dresses*."

Kristy glanced out of the attic window. "The rain's letting up a little, Jason," she said. "After lunch perhaps you and I can go over to that playground."

"Martha and me, too," Karen said.

"Karen, you can do something with the others this afternoon," Kristy said in her I-mean-what-I-say voice. "Jason and I are going alone this time."

"Oh, bother!" Karen said.

Just then I felt a gentle tap on my arm. It was

Dawn. "Mary Anne," she whispered to me, "before we go back downstairs, Claud and I are going to try to work out which bedroom was Lydia's."

"And find the stairs to the widow's walk," Claud added.

I couldn't imagine doing such an unbearably scary thing.

"Do you want to come with us?" Dawn asked.

"No, I do not," I said emphatically. "And I don't want you to go either. Please, let's all go back downstairs together."

"We'll be down in a minute," Dawn said. But I noticed she didn't look too relaxed herself. She and Claud went down the corridor while Kristy and I took the kids downstairs. Kristy went on with the kids to the ground floor while I waited in our corridor for Dawn and Claud. I was wondering how they could do such a scary thing, when suddenly I heard feet running along the floor above me. Did they belong to two people? Or to two people being chased by a third? What if our villain were chasing Claud and Dawn?

Footsteps were pounding down the stairs. Even though I was terrified I opened the door to the stairwell. Dawn and Claud practically tumbled down the last few stairs. As soon as they were in the corridor I banged the door shut.

"What did you see?" I managed to say.

128

"The cat's up there," Claud answered. "At first we thought it was a person . . . or ghost."

"I think that cat *is* a ghost," Dawn said.

"Or belongs to one," Claud added.

We shuddered.

"But we had time to work out that the doors to the widow's walk and to the bedrooms at the back of the house, including the one that was Lydia's, are locked," Dawn said.

I couldn't help wondering if Georgio had keys to those rooms too.

12th CHAPTER

Kristy

Tuesday
11:45 p.m.

I really meant what I said last
night at our emergency BSC meeting.
We have to forget about ghost-
busting and focus on our baby-sitting
job. If we spend our nights worrying
about ghosts, it's going to be harder
and harder to spend our days
taking care of kids. (I am already
exhausted.) But here I am tonight,
wide awake and scared out of my
wits again.

130

"Come on, Jason, grab your glove. We're going to the playground." It was after lunch on Tuesday and I was determined to help Jason Menders meet some boys of his own age.

"But it's still raining," he protested.

"Then we'll see what the kids do here on a rainy day. I bet they're in the recreation barn."

"I don't want to go," Jason said. "Those kids are stuck-up."

"Would you rather stay here and play dressing-up with Karen and Martha?" I asked.

That did it. Jason ran upstairs and came back with his glove. "Let's go to the playground," he said.

The rain was still coming down hard when we reached the playground. No one was outside, so we headed for the rec barn. It was quite small— about the size of a double garage.

I was pleased to see that the place was filled with the boys we'd seen playing softball the day before. Four of them were playing Ping-Pong. They looked at us when we came in, but didn't say hello or anything. Another group was sitting on an old sofa playing a hand-held computer game. More kids were sitting at a table playing a board game.

Not one kid greeted us. Also, they didn't seem to be having much fun. I thought they were probably sick of being cooped up because of the rain.

131

Kristy

"Do you know how to play Ping-Pong?" I whispered to Jason.

"There's a Ping-Pong table in the cellar of my building in Boston," Jason whispered back. "I'm the best player on the block."

"OK," I said. "Ask them if you can play."

"I can't do THAT!" Jason hissed.

"Of course you can!"

Jason turned his baseball cap back-to-front, handed me his glove and ball, and walked to the Ping-Pong table. "Can I play the winner?" he asked. I was so proud of him.

But no one would have been proud of those other kids. "We're not playing for points," one of them said. Not another word out of any of them. They kept hitting that Ping-Pong ball to and fro, to and fro, and ignoring Jason.

It was time for more aggressive action. I walked over to the table. "Hi," I said, "I'm Kristy Thomas."

"And I'm Jason Menders," Jason said.

None of them said a word to us. But I heard a boy behind me say, "The summer boy's got a *nanny*." I was glad Jason was on the other side of the Ping-Pong table and didn't hear that comment.

"I coach a softball team in Stoneybrook, Connecticut," I announced to anyone who would listen. "I wish my team was in Reese with me,

132

because if they were I'd challenge you guys to a game. Who's your coach?"

"Our coach is away," a red-haired kid muttered. "He went to be a counsellor at a residential camp."

"Oh. I suppose if he were around he'd be able to help you guys with that problem you have making the double play."

"And your hitting," Jason added.

"What's the matter with our hitting?" a tough-looking kid asked.

I dodged his question by saying, "I suppose you're not playing in a league or anything if you haven't got a coach."

"And I noticed you only have one pitcher," Jason added. (He was doing fine!)

"Our other pitcher went to the residential camp, too," one of the computer game kids muttered.

"And Chad was no help," the red-haired kid said.

"Who's Chad?" I asked.

"He was our best pitcher last summer. But he's a summer kid. They all leave in September. And September's when the regional softball playoff is. We lost last year 'cause Chad wasn't here. So we don't play with summer people or tourists any more. It's our rule."

I began to get the picture. These boys were avoiding Jason because they thought he was one of those "summer people" who leave in September (and have nannies).

"I might move here," Jason told them. "If I like it. My uncle died and left us his house."

"Yeah?" one of the Ping-Pong players asked. "You'd go to school here and everything?"

"Yes," Jason answered. "If I like it."

"I'm not moving here like Jason," I said. "But I'll be around for another week. Then I have to go back to my own softball team. My team is called the Krushers. What's your team called?"

"We haven't got a name," the red-haired kid said.

"That's too bad," I told him. "I suppose you haven't got T-shirts either."

"Who'd want to sponsor *us*?" I heard one boy whisper to another.

I looked out of the window. The rain was letting up.

I tossed Jason his glove across the Ping-Pong table. I made sure it was a toss he would really have to reach for. He caught it back-handed. And all those guys saw him do it.

"I watched you play yesterday. And you know what I saw?" I asked them.

All eyes were on me. No one was pretending to play a game. No one was hitting a Ping-Pong ball. At last I had their undivided attention. I said, "I saw a lot of talent on that field. As a matter of fact I saw so much talent that I want to help you. I'm willing to help you." For good measure I added, "For free."

They looked at one another. These guys needed a leader so badly they couldn't bring themselves to turn me down—even though I'm a girl and they were the kind of boys who'd ordinarily have trouble with that. Which, of course, made me want to play ball with them more than ever. "I'm glad you agree," I told them. "You won't regret it. Let's start by getting out on that muddy field and playing some ball."

There was a chorus of "yeahs" and "OKs" as kids grabbed gloves and bats and hurried out of the door.

Jason flashed me a thank-you smile as we followed them.

That night, when the kids were asleep, Claudia and Dawn came into my room. Dawn said, "We've got an idea about how to clear up the mystery of the ghosts once and for all."

"But we need your help," Claud said. "And Mary Anne's."

When I heard their idea I thought we might be able to put an end to the ghost talk that very night. It sounded dangerous. But I agreed to it. (Mistake Number 1!)

Mary Anne and I were supposed to go outside at nine-thirty and watch the mansion to see if the third-floor lights went on again. Meanwhile,

Claudia and Dawn would be spying in the third-floor corridor to see if anyone else (meaning the one person who has a key to the third floor—Georgio) came upstairs.

When nine-thirty arrived, Mary Anne and I were hidden behind some bushes. We had a perfect view of the back of the mansion.

"I could never in a million years do what Dawn and Claud are doing," Mary Anne told me. "I'd have a heart attack from fear." (Mistake Number 2 was thinking that our job wasn't as scary as Claud's and Dawn's.)

Later Claud told us that she and Dawn both felt terrified as they went upstairs. What if someone—or some*thing*—was already up there? But they peered around the corner into the corridor and didn't see anyone. So far, the coast was clear.

"I wish Lydia's room wasn't locked," Dawn whispered to Claudia.

"We could look through the keyhole," Claud said.

Dawn volunteered to do the looking.

The keyhole provided Dawn with a view of the room. She took a quick look around and reported to Claud. "No one's there, unless they're in the wardrobe."

Claud and Dawn hid themselves in the corridor alcove and waited to see if anyone went into, or out of, that room.

136

Meanwhile Mary Anne was keeping an eye on the back door to see if anyone went into the house. And I was watching the row of bedroom windows on the third floor. Suddenly I saw a light go on in the same room in which I'd seen it the night before. "Mary Anne," I whispered. "Look."

The light stayed on for about two minutes and then went off. During the time it was on we checked to see if it was caused by a reflection from the lighthouse beam. But it was a clear night and the lighthouse was dark. Besides, the light in Lydia's room looked identical to the warm glow given off by all the other electric lights in the house.

We stood still and clutched one another while we watched that window. The light went back on after a couple of minutes. A few minutes later it went off again.

Mary Anne was whispering, "Where are Dawn and Claud? Oh, Kristy, I'm so *worried*." I tried to calm her down but I was pretty scared myself, and I think she could tell.

When the light had stayed off for five minutes, we decided it was time to go in and tell Claud and Dawn what we'd seen. "I hope Georgio didn't find them spying on him," Mary Anne whispered to me as we walked towards the house. A moment later, Mary Anne cried out and hid her face in one hand while she pointed to the top of the mansion

137

with the other. "Tell me I didn't see that," she mumbled into my sweatshirt.

I saw a figure in white walking on the widow's walk. I knew I saw it. It wasn't my imagination. Even when the ghostly figure had disappeared, I was shaking with fright.

"It's gone," I told Mary Anne.

I grabbed her hand and we ran all the way to the mansion and into the kitchen. Elton was sitting at the table reading the newspaper. He looked up and asked, "What's wrong, girls? You look like you've seen a ghost."

"We didn't," I said quickly. "We're in a hurry." It wasn't till later that I wondered why I didn't tell him that we *had* seen a ghost.

We raced up the stairs to the second floor. I was terrified. If Georgio was trying to scare us, he was going to a lot of trouble to do it. What else would he do? How dangerous was he? Then again, if the ghosts were real (which I didn't *really* believe), they were probably evil ghosts. Dangerous ghosts.

When we saw Dawn and Claud in our corridor we all hugged each other. Dawn and Claudia were pale. We all rushed off to Mary Anne's room to talk. Mary Anne started crying, I suppose with relief that they (and we) were safe.

First I told Claud and Dawn about the figure in white. Then we went over everything that had happened, step by step. Claud and Dawn had also

138

seen the light in the room. The corridor was dark, so the light glowed through the keyhole. (They were both too frightened to actually look through the keyhole.)

"It's Lydia's room," Claud said. "I just know it. And I'm pretty sure Georgio isn't responsible for any of this. We would have seen him."

"Unless he was hiding in a wardrobe in the room," Dawn said.

"What about the figure in white?" Claud asked. "Georgio couldn't have been in both places at once."

"Perhaps he's got a woman accomplice," Dawn suggested. "Kristy said the figure in white looked like a woman."

I could tell that Claud was hoping with all her heart that Georgio wasn't our villain. And she probably didn't want to hear that he had a female accomplice. Poor Claud.

We were so frightened that we whispered our goodnights.

A little later, while I was trying to fall asleep, I went over the day's—and night's—events and asked myself questions. What would happen next? Who was doing all these creepy things? And most mysterious of all, why?

The wind—or was it a ghost?—rattled the window.

I lay awake listening to my heartbeat. At last I closed my eyes and tried to fall asleep.

Kristy

I soon felt a thump on my legs. I opened my eyes and stared into yellow-green eyes. I thought of Dracula, and bats, and stories I'd heard of campers waking up to find a snake crawling over them. As my eyes became used to the darkness I was sure a big bat was sitting on my legs. But when the "bat" hss-sshed, and jumped over me and off the bed, I realized it was Spooky.

I saw him run through the bathroom towards Mary Anne's room. I jumped out of bed and followed him. If Spooky did to Mary Anne what he'd just done to me, she *definitely* would have a heart attack.

I opened the door onto the corridor, hoping Spooky would leave. He did. Then I checked to be sure that Mary Anne was still asleep. She was. But it was a very long time before I fell asleep.

Mallory

Jessi and I are booked solid. Sorry, guys, but we had to turn down quite a few jobs — eight, to be exact. That was on Monday. Today, Wednesday, not many people called.

We miss you all and can't wait until you come home and things go back to normal.

"Mal, I don't feel like being chairman today," Jessi told me. "You can do it."

We were in Claud's room for our Wednesday BSC meeting, and we were pretty tired from all the babysitting we'd been doing. We were the *only* ones at the meeting. Shannon had a dentist's appointment and Logan was working at the Rosebud.

"I don't want to be chairman either," I said. "As there's only only two of us, we don't really need one."

Jessi agreed with a nod. "Let's take turns phoning the people who left messages," she suggested.

"OK," I said.

I pressed the play button. I had a piece of paper and a pencil ready to write down the names and phone numbers of callers. But that wasn't necessary for the first message. It was from Jessi.

"This is me—Jessi—just making sure the machine is on and working."

"That was a good idea," I told her. My mood lifted a little. Maybe we weren't doing so badly after all.

"Thanks," Jessi said.

"*Beep. Beep. Beep.*" Three beeps meant there were no more messages.

"I suppose my message was the only one," Jessi concluded glumly.

I sat next to her on the bed. "Look on the

142

bright side," I said. "We won't have to turn down so many people."

"Maybe they're waiting till the meeting to call," Jessi suggested.

But fifteen minutes passed and the phone didn't ring once.

"Nothing seems right since the others left," Jessi said. "I'm tired from so many babysitting jobs. And Becca's sulking because I haven't got time to teach her how to Rollerblade."

"My mum's really grumpy with me, too," I told Jessi. "I explained that it's not my fault all the sitters left town. But she said we should have planned it better. I promised her I'd take all my brothers and sisters to Celebrate America! Day."

Jessi and I were looking forward to Celebrate America! It was Stoneybrook's big summer celebration, starting with a parade in the morning followed by a barbecue picnic at the playground. During the afternoon there'd be games from colonial times, and hands-on activities, such as kite-making.

Jessi looked at the record book. "But you're scheduled to take the Rodowskys to Celebrate America!"

"Mrs Rodowsky is going to be at the fair running the dunking booth, and my mother will be at the kite booth. As they'll be there, they decided it was OK for me to look after all the kids. I just have to keep ten kids safe and happy!"

143

It sounded like a tough job even if Mrs Rodowsky and my mum were going to be there.

"I'd help you, but I'm overbooked too," Jessi said. "I'm going to take the Braddocks, the Marshalls *and* Becca. Mrs Braddock and my mother are working together on the make-your-own rag doll booth. So there'll be a lot of adults around that we know. But it's still a huge amount of work."

At last the BSC phone rang.

It was Mrs Prezzioso wanting a sitter on Celebrate America! Day for Jenny, Andrea and the twins.

I looked at the list of times Shannon and Logan were available to take jobs. Neither of them had listed that day.

"Sorry, Mrs Prezzioso," I said. "There aren't any sitters available."

When I'd rung off I told Jessi, "You know what Mrs Prezzioso said? 'But I thought the whole point of the club was to have sitters *available*. I'm very disappointed.'"

"I think a lot of people are disappointed with us," Jessi said with a sigh. "What are we going to do, Mal? We've ruined the club."

"Maybe we should make posters and put them up around town," I said. "Or send a letter to our clients."

"By the time they get the letter Kristy and

144

everybody will be home and things will be back to normal," Jessi pointed out.

"Or ruined for ever," I added darkly.

"We could put posters up straight away," Jessi said.

We talked about the poster idea, but eventually realized that it would be too hard to explain what had happened to the BSC in a few words.

As we left Claud's room I remembered all the wonderful meetings we'd been to there. This hadn't been one of them. Would we ever have good meetings again? Or had we ruined the BSC for ever?

14th CHAPTER

Mary Anne

Wednesday
5:00 p.m.

I don't believe in ghosts. And I don't believe this mansion is haunted. I do believe that if we are thorough in our investigation (and don't jump to conclusions) we will figure out what's really going on here.

146

"Mary Anne, take me to see the boats now. *Please!*"

I opened my eyes. It was Wednesday morning and Andrew had climbed on to my bed to wake me up.

"Oh, goody! You're awake," he said. "Kristy's asleep and I want to see the boats. OK?"

"Is it a sunny day?" I asked, rubbing my eyes.

"Very sunny," he answered. "There'll be *lots* of boats. This many." He held up both hands to show me his ten fingers.

I explained to Andrew that our day's plan was to spend as much time as we could outdoors, starting at the community swimming pool. "After that we'll go to the harbour and see the boats. But first we'll swim. OK?"

"I can swim," Andrew said. "I'll pretend I'm a boat."

I gave him a hug. Andrew's a great kid.

Jill and Dawn came into the room. "We've got our swimsuits on under our shorts and T-shirts," Jill informed me. "And we've both got blue T-shirts, see?"

I reminded myself that we *had* to help Jill make some friends of her own age in Reese.

After breakfast Kristy and Jason went off to the ballfield. Lionel said he'd stay at home and read *Dracula* (the novel by Bram Stoker). He wanted to read the novel before he saw the play. The rest of us walked the kilometre to Reese community

147

pool. It was a huge pool near the sea. That morning the pool was divided in half with a buoy rope. One half was reserved for the members of the swimming team who were waiting at the poolside in their matching navy and white suits. The other half of the pool was open for general free swimming. There was also a kiddie pool, which was perfect for Andrew-the-Boat.

I thought if both Jill and Martha signed up for the swimming team, they'd be involved in an activity they could share while meeting kids of their own age.

"Girls," I said, "let's go and find out about the swimming team."

"Martha, *you* should be in the swimming team," Karen exclaimed. "I bet that's a *great* way to meet people."

I noticed that Martha put as much distance between herself and Karen as she could without being rude. Dawn managed to persuade Karen to stay with Claud and Andrew, then she and I took Jill and Martha to the swimming team side of the pool.

We sat near the lifeguard stand and watched the team go through their warming-up exercises. Dawn told Jill she used to be in a swimming team in California and how much she liked it. Meanwhile, I talked to Martha about how much fun it was to swim. And she told me she'd had swimming lessons at the day camp she went to in Boston.

When the team was practising the butterfly stroke, Jill proudly announced, "I can do that."

"Can Martha?" I asked.

"Yes, she's a good swimmer too," Jill said. "Especially for a little kid. We both passed intermediate."

I winked at Dawn. She smiled back. Our idea just might work.

Two coaches were conducting the swimming team session. I decided that the one with the whistle and clipboard was the head coach. "Is it too late for kids to sign up for the team?" I asked her.

"No. Anyone who's passed Beginners can join," she told me.

"I'm asking for two sisters who might like to join," I said. "One is ten, the other seven."

"Ask them to come over," she said.

I went back to Dawn and the girls. "If you've passed Beginners you can be in the team."

Jill leaped up. "All right!" she said. "Come on, Dawn. You and I can join."

"Jill, you know I'm going back to Stoneybrook next week," Dawn said. "I can't join. But you and Martha could. And I'd watch your practices every day till I leave."

Jill sat down again. "I'm not doing it if you aren't, Dawn," she said emphatically.

149

Mary Anne

"Martha, you could join anyway," I said. "I know you like swimming."

"If Jill doesn't do it, I won't," Martha whispered to me.

Just then the instructor approached us. "You must be the new girls," she said to Martha and Jill. "We could really use you on the team."

Jill said, "No, thanks."

Martha looked at the ground and didn't say anything.

"Martha and Jill are still thinking about it," Dawn told the coach.

"We're having a mini-fair tomorrow—a fund-raiser, put together by the kids, with games and a cake stall," she said. "Why don't you all come? It'd be a great way to meet the other kids on the team and talk to them about it."

We said thanks and that we would be there.

"Hope to see you tomorrow, Martha and Jill," the coach said as she went back to her team.

Just then I noticed Karen making her way towards us. The last thing Martha needed now was Karen's over-exuberant efforts.

"Let's go back to the other side of the pool and do some swimming," I said. While Dawn took the girls into the water, I sat by the kiddie pool where Claudia was watching Andrew, and told Claud about the mini-fair.

"That sounds like fun," Claud said. "I wonder

150

Mary Anne

what we could do to help? I know! Maybe they'd let us have a face-painting booth."

When the swimming team practice was over, Claud and I told the coach our idea. She thought it was terrific.

Then we told our kids.

"I want Claudia to make me a cat," Karen said. "What do you want to be, Martha?"

Martha said, "I don't know."

"I want to be a frog," Andrew said.

Karen asked Jill how she wanted her face painted.

"However Dawn has hers," Jill answered.

After swimming and playing around at the pool, we were all pretty hungry. So we went to the harbour and bought lunch from an outdoor stand, then sat near the dock and watched the boats while we ate. Andrew was thrilled.

When we'd finished our lunch I told Dawn, "The historical society is open this afternoon. I'd like to go over there for a while."

"The girls are pretty tired from swimming," Dawn said. "And Andrew could do with a nap. Claud and I can take them back to the house and you can go alone." I thought that was an excellent idea. I had some serious research to do, and it'd be easier to do it without babysitting responsibilities.

The historical society is in an old brick house off the Main Street. The door was open, so I

151

walked inside. It was dark and cool. After the bright light and heat of the outdoors, it felt wonderful.

A tiny white-haired woman was sitting at a small table in the front hall. "Good afternoon," she chirped. "May I help you?"

"I'm interested in learning more about the old houses around here," I told her. "This seems like a good place to start."

"Indeed it is," she said. She stood up. "I'm Eleanor Butterfield and I'll do what I can to assist you."

I explained that I was mostly interested in the Randolph mansion. "I'm hoping you have some old architectural plans of the house," I said.

She led me into the front parlour, which serves as the historical society library. "I believe we have something in the vertical files," she said. I followed her to a filing cabinet.

While she was going through old documents, I told her that I'd heard about *A Historical Tour of Reese* by Millicent Ellsworth.

"Oh, yes," she said. "But Millicent got a bit carried away with her stories. She had a flair for the dramatic."

When I asked what she meant by that, Mrs Butterfield explained, "Millicent's dates for births, deaths, fires and so on were all accurate. But when it came to personal stories, she was known to exaggerate and even veer from the truth."

I told her the story of Reginald and Mary Randolph that Claudia had read in *A Historical Tour of Reese*.

"Well, my dear," Mrs Butterfield said, "some people like to believe those stories. I suppose it's good for tourism. The facts about Mary Randolph are these. She had two children and six or so grandchildren. Her son and his family lived at the mansion with her. It was a lively place in those days. I've seen references in diaries and journals to parties and hunts and all sorts of joyous events at the mansion in the years that Mary was a widow. And I've seen her name listed among those who did volunteer work at the local hospital and for the Seamen's Widows and Orphans Society. I expect Mary Randolph did indeed grieve for her husband. Perhaps she even took to the widow's walk now and again. But she wasn't 'flung to her death' from it in a storm. Town records inform us she died in her sleep."

Mrs Butterfield pulled a file from the cabinet and handed it to me. "Here we are," she said. "Architectural drawings of the Randolph mansion. You're not allowed to take this file out of the room, but you may spend as much time as you like with it here."

Mrs Butterfield went back to her desk in the hall. I sat at a table in the library and studied the

original floor plans. Once I got used to the way
they were drawn I looked for familiar things such
as the kitchen, our bedrooms and the staircase to
the third floor. My objective was to see if there
was anything in the drawings that I didn't
recognize—such as a secret passage.

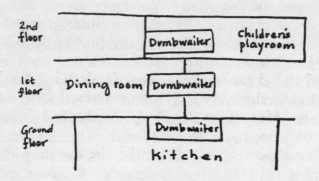

I noticed that what looked like a cupboard on
the ground-floor drawing was labelled "dumbwaiter." It was there on the second-floor drawing
too. This one was in the "children's playroom". I
studied the location of the children's playroom. It
was Dawn's bedroom.

Mrs Butterfield came back to the library to see
how I was doing and to ask if I had any questions.

"I was wondering if you could tell me what a
dumbwaiter is," I said.

"Why, yes," she said. "It's a small lift used to
move food from one floor to another." She traced

the plan with a forefinger. "In the Randolph mansion it went from the kitchen to the children's playroom, where the nanny would serve the younger children their meals. As you can imagine, a dumbwaiter came in quite handy. You see, trays of food could be sent up, and dirty dishes sent down, without all that stair-climbing. Just with the pull of a rope."

"So there are doors that open onto the dumbwaiter in each of those eating rooms?" I asked.

"That's correct," she said.

When I'd copied the parts of the drawing that I wanted to show my fellow detectives, I took the file to Mrs Butterfield. "Thanks," I said. "You've been very helpful."

"You know what's curious?" she asked.

"What?"

"As you can see, we don't have many visitors here. But you're the second person this month who's asked for information about the Randolph mansion."

"Who's the other person?" I asked. (I thought it would be Mr or Mrs Menders, after they'd inherited the estate.)

"She didn't tell me her name," Mrs Butterfield answered. "But I do remember that she spoke with a thick accent." An accent? Well, that definitely ruled out the Menderses.

I left the historical society feeling both pleased and puzzled.

Claudia

Wednesday
11 p.m.

I am so dispointed in Georgio. I hate that he acts like he's my freind (when all he wants is to steel.) I feel sory for his grandparrents.

By the way, remined me never to go to a scarey play when I'm in the midle of solving a mystery!

I was sitting on a garden chair sketching the grove of pine trees.

"Hi!"

It was Georgio.

"Hi," I replied cautiously.

He sat on the grass next to me. "It looks like you've got the afternoon off too," he said.

"Everyone's having a quiet hour."

"How would you like go for a quiet walk with me?" he asked. He held up a bunch of herbs. "I'm taking my grandparents some herbs from their old kitchen garden."

"Your grandparents who were caretakers here?"

He nodded. "Do you want to come?"

"OK." I closed my sketchpad. "I'll tell the others where I'm going. I'll be right back."

Even though Georgio gave me the creeps I knew I should go with him. I could ask his grandparents about the mansion, and work on finding the answer to what had become the biggest question of all for me: is Georgio Trono the one who's trying to frighten us, and if so, why?

Despite my doubts about Georgio, I enjoyed our walk to his grandparents' flat. Georgio loves his home town, and I enjoyed hearing about what growing up in Reese was like for him. We passed his grammar school, and the fire station where his father and grandfather served as volunteer

157

firefighters. As we walked through the park where the Founders' Day celebration would be held, he asked me, "How's that float coming along?"

"We're thinking of a historical theme," I told him. "And wearing some of the old clothes we found in the attic."

"I don't think you should go up there."

"Why not?"

"I told you," he answered sternly. "No one's used that part of the house in years. I'm not sure it's safe. I'm sorry that I opened it up for you yesterday."

I'd spent all morning in that attic the day before, and I hadn't seen anything that looked dangerous. What was Georgio's *real* reason for not wanting us snooping around on the third floor?

Georgio announced that we'd reached his grandparents' house. The Tronos were pleased to see Georgio and to meet me. They served us homemade lemonade and fabulous brownies. And I didn't have to bring up the subject of the mansion . . . because *they* did.

"That's quite a big house, isn't it?" Mr Trono said to me.

"It certainly is," I replied. "And beautiful. Do you miss it?"

"Oh, yes." Mrs Trono passed me the plate of brownies. "But mostly we miss Mr Randolph. He was a fine gentleman to work for, and a dear, dear friend. We took care of him to the very end."

"How did he die?" I asked.

"Oh, it was a long illness. He didn't know us towards the end. He was always mumbling on about the past, the way dying people sometimes do."

"About the past in the mansion?" I asked. This could be *very* interesting.

"He did mention the attic once or twice," Mr Trono said.

Georgio interrupted. "Claudia isn't that interested in Mr Randolph, Gramps. She wants to know how people dressed. Things like that. For a float she's doing for the parade."

Georgio was trying to change the subject because we were talking about the attic!

"I think the Menderses would be interested in knowing what their uncle was talking about on his deathbed," I said firmly. "And so am I."

"I suppose they would," Mrs Trono said. "Mr Randolph often said he wanted his 'treasure from the attic'. But nothing he said in those last days made sense, so I've never believed there was any real treasure in the attic."

Treasure in the attic! That would explain a lot.

"I think you're right, Grandma," Georgio put in. "Those were just the mumblings of a dying man. There's nothing in the attic." (How did he know what was up there?)

I wanted to ask the Tronos about the dumbwaiter. But as I didn't want Georgio to suspect that I was doing detective work, I had to be careful how I brought up the subject. "What I like best about big old houses," I began, "are all the special features like verandahs and butlers' pantries and dumbwaiters."

"Well, the mansion certainly has everything you've mentioned," Mr Trono said.

"I haven't noticed a dumbwaiter," I said.

"Oh, the dumbwaiter has been covered up for years. We never used it. Mr Randolph always liked to eat in the dining room off the verandah."

"And when he was ill we carried him his meals," Mrs Trono added. She patted my hand kindly. "The dumbwaiter could be dangerous, dear, so do stay away from it."

Georgio stood up. "We have to go now," he said abruptly.

In a minute we were all standing at the front door. "What a lovely visit," Mrs Trono said. "Claudia, I do hope you'll come and visit us again some time."

I said thank you and goodbye, and we left. As I walked down the street with Georgio I thought over the evidence I'd gathered. I was more certain than ever that he was the "ghost" trying to scare us sitters and the kids. And now I know why he was doing it. He wanted to find Mr Randolph's treasure and keep it for himself.

Wednesday was our night off. We had big plans—pizza and the summer stock production of *Dracula*. I put on my black gauze skirt and a red tank top, and tied my white silk bomber jacket around my waist. Then I put on my aeroplane earrings. Dawn, Kristy and Mary Anne came into my room to keep me company.

I told them everything that had happened at the Tronos', including the part about Georgio not wanting his grandparents to tell me anything.

"So our 'ghost' probably isn't a ghost," Mary Anne said.

Dawn wanted to review all the clues again, but it was time to leave.

I loved having the evening off. And—believe it or not—Lionel was part of the fun. On the way to town he made us laugh so much we couldn't stop. He would speak in different accents and we'd try to guess where he was supposed to be from. I was the worst at guessing. When he put on a Scottish accent I thought it was Australian.

We took a big booth in the pizza parlour and ordered a pizza deluxe. While we were waiting for the pizza, we quizzed Lionel about his ghostly activities at the beginning of the week.

"Did you play corridor ghost two nights in a row?" Dawn asked.

"Yes," he confessed.

"What colour candle did you carry the *first* night?" I asked.

"Orange. But when I saw you lot inspecting the carpet, I realized the wax had dripped. So I bought white candles—dripless ones. A ghost wouldn't drip wax, would it?"

"That's debatable," I answered.

"Lionel, where did you find the orange candle you used that first night?" Dawn asked.

"In the gardener's shed, where Georgio keeps his tools," he said matter-of-factly. "And speak of the devil. . ."

Lionel was looking towards the front door. Georgio had come in and spotted us. Or had he spotted us and then come in? In any case, he strode over to our table and treated us like long-lost friends.

After everyone had said hello, Georgio asked, "Mind if I join you?"

Naturally, we couldn't object. As we made room for Georgio, Lionel told him, "We were just talking about you."

"I hope you only said nice things," Georgio replied. He was looking at me when he said that. I felt myself blush.

Mary Anne said, "We're going to see *Dracula* tonight." Mary Anne was trying to change the subject, but her effort boomeranged, because Georgio said, "I know some of the guys working

162

on that production. Do you mind if I come with you?"

I wanted to say, "I *do* mind. Leave us alone!" But how could I do that? Especially when Georgio told us he'd be happy to introduce Lionel to his friends who were working on the play.

We spent the rest of our time at the pizza parlour making plans for our Founders' Day float. Georgio insisted that *he* should bring the clothes down from the attic for us, and he repeated what he had said to me at his grandparents', that the third floor wasn't safe.

I noticed Mary Anne's eyes growing round with fright and Kristy looking suspiciously at Georgio. They were probably thinking what I was thinking. Get me away from this guy!

Going to the play was scary beyond words. I didn't know who to be more afraid of in that darkened theatre—Count Dracula on the stage or Georgio off the stage (he was sitting next to me).

By the time we left for home Lionel was hyper-excited. Georgio had introduced him to the teenage ushers at the theatre. They seemed to like Lionel, and said if he stopped by before the performance the following night he could meet all the people involved in the production and help hand out programmes. I was keyed up, too: freaked-out by the dark, moonless night, Lionel's nonstop imitation of Count Dracula, and Georgio (who insisted on walking next to me all the way home).

When we reached the mansion, Lionel raced ahead. He probably couldn't wait to tell his family about the theatre group and the contacts he'd made. As the rest of us walked round to the back door, Georgio pointed to the third floor. "Look at that," he said. "You lot must have left a light on up there."

"Yeah," I said, "I suppose so."

By then I think we'd all decided that somehow he was responsible for that light. So none of us would give him the satisfaction of seeming scared.

Then we all saw it—a flutter of white fabric moving across the widow's walk. Mary Anne let out a frightened squeak and Dawn gasped. Otherwise we remained calm. Or pretended we were calm. I wanted to scream and run all the way home to Stoneybrook.

Naturally, Georgio saw the figure in white too, but he acted surprised (the rat!). "Something weird is going on here," Georgio whispered to me. "I don't want to frighten anyone, but, Claudia, I want you to promise me you won't go to the third floor again."

"OK," I said. "I promise." *I* knew what was weird. Georgio. I was so disappointed in him. I'd hoped he was a nice guy.

That night I slept in Dawn's room again. I heard the woman's scream in the wall that she'd

164

told me about. I reminded myself, it's just Georgio's female accomplice, not a ghost. But it wasn't all that comforting. I couldn't help wondering what Georgio's next step might be. I was still lying awake, feeling upset, and frightened of more things than I could keep track of.

ANDREW

DEAR DADDY,
RIBB-ID. I'M A FROG. I SAW A BOAT.
X X OO
ANDREW

I went to the mini-fair. Claudia painted faces.

Karen was a cat.

Martha was a mouse.

Jill was a teenager.

Guess what I was? Rib-bid.

Claudia made lots of kids look like animals. She gave all the money to the swimming team.

Martha made a new friend today. Karen didn't help her at all. Martha's friend is Jody. Jody is in the swimming team. Jody wanted to be a mouse like Martha.

My babysitters are silly. At the fair they followed ladies who talked like Mary Poppins. Kristy said, "Andrew, I'm looking for someone, but I don't want her to know. It's a secret."

Some of the people we followed were baby-sitters. Mary Poppins was a babysitter, too. But some of the other ladies were on holiday.

I asked Mary Anne, "Why do people talk funny on holiday?" She said people come to America with their "accents". When I go on a journey I take a suitcase.

Claudia asked one lady, "Do you know the way to Randolph Mansion?"

A silly-billy question! Claudia knows how to get to the mansion. We all know the way back. The lady thought it was a silly-billy question, too. She said, "No. Should I?"

Claudia told Kristy, "I give up."

Dawn

I think we did a better job today at helping the Menders kids. Martha made a friend at the fair, and Jill spent an afternoon without me (a major accomplishment!) The biggest surprise of all is that Lionel and Jason have a common interest. If we could just persuade Jill and Martha to join the swim team, I think all four Menders kids would be

Dawn

happy — at least for the rest of the summer.

Now our biggest (and toughest) job is to identify the villains (or ghosts?) in the Menderses' new home. By the time we leave Reese this mystery must be solved!

I learned something about myself today. I hate being trapped in small, dark spaces!

"Dawn, do I have to go to the mini-fair if I don't want to?" Jason asked me.

Apart from Jason, all the kids were excited about going to the fair, particularly because we were going to run a face-painting booth. When I told Kristy what Jason had said, we agreed that Jason shouldn't be forced to go, and that I'd stay with him. I had a theory that Jill might have a better chance of making new friends at the mini-fair if I wasn't there. Kristy agreed, adding, "I also want Jason to get used to going to the playground without me."

When the others had left for the fair, I turned to Jason and said, "Let's go to the ballfield and you can play softball."

"Not without Kristy," he said.

"Kristy's going home in a few days," I reminded him. "What will you do then?"

169

Jason shrugged his shoulders.

"OK, well, how about playing catch here for a while?" I suggested. I decided that after we'd played, I'd bring up the idea of going to the playground again.

We threw the ball to and fro. I could tell that Jason was rather bored playing with me (softball is *not* my sport). So when I saw Lionel, I threw the ball to him. The ball didn't go where Lionel could easily reach it, but still he caught it. I was surprised—and impressed.

Lionel threw the ball to Jason, and Jason threw it back to him. "Lionel," I called out, "I've got to go inside for a minute. Will you play with Jason till I come back?"

"I think I'm doing that," he said.

The brothers were playing together for the first time that week. Inside I made fresh lemonade. When I went back outside with it, Lionel was showing Jason how to throw a knuckleball.

While they were guzzling the lemonade, I said, "Lionel, you seem to know a lot about softball."

"His team won the Massachusetts Little League championship," Jason said proudly. "He's got a big trophy."

"That's great, Lionel!" I exclaimed. "So why don't *you* take Jason to the ballfield?"

Jason's eyes grew wide with excitement. "Would you?" he asked his brother.

"I suppose I could," Lionel answered. "But I'm not a sporty type any more. I'm an actor."

"Think of it as a part in a play," I suggested, "and act the role of a guy who loves softball and is going to the ballfield with his younger brother."

"Hey," he said, "not a bad idea."

I noticed that Lionel was wearing white linen trousers and a beige short-sleeved shirt. "And don't forget your costume," I suggested. "You might want to dress the part, too."

"Right again," he said. "Back in five minutes."

A few minutes later Lionel appeared before us in cut-off jeans, a T-shirt that read "Boston Red Sox", and a baseball cap turned sideways. "It's all in the details," he told me.

When they'd gone, I was alone at the mansion. At first I thought I'd go to the mini-fair and catch up with the others. Then I decided this was a perfect opportunity to work on our mystery. I lay in the hammock reading through our holiday notebook, reviewing clues, and doing some strategic planning. By the time I'd worked out what our next step should be, Lionel and Jason had come back.

I met them on the lawn halfway between the hammock and the house. They were each carrying a litre-bottle of lemonade. Jason was grinning from ear to ear. "Lionel's going to be our coach!" he announced.

Dawn

"Lionel," I exclaimed, "that's wonderful! It's absolutely fabulous."

"Now we've got the best coach of any team," Jason said.

Lionel gulped from his bottle. "It's a tough role," he told me, wiping his mouth with the back of his hand. "But I can handle it." He gave his brother a friendly punch on the arm. "Right, buddy?"

When Jason went running off to the kitchen for a snack, Lionel told me, "This'll work out fine. Playing softball will help keep me in shape, which is very important in acting. And I'll still be free at night to work at the theatre." I had a feeling Lionel wasn't going to be bored in Reese after all.

During the next half an hour everyone came home and congregated on the verandah. We admired Claud's face paintings. Then Lionel, who'd showered and changed back into his white linen trousers, left for the theatre. The parents took the rest of the kids for a late-afternoon walk along the beach. The Coopers were out buying groceries. So at last the four babysitters were on their own at the mansion.

I asked Kristy if they'd traced the woman with the accent at the mini-fair. I knew they'd planned to do a little sleuthing while they were there.

"*The* woman?!" Kristy exclaimed. "We found a *dozen* women with accents." She explained that some of the wealthy people who spend the

172

summer in Reese have European nannies, who speak English with an accent.

"And a tour group of women from England were at the fair," Claud added. "They've got heavy British accents."

"And don't forget the two French families who are here for the summer," Mary Anne said.

"The result of the BSC Mini-Fair Spy Operation," Kristy concluded, "was that we looked pretty foolish. Even Andrew noticed."

"Well, I've got a plan," I said. "As everyone's out, this is the perfect opportunity to have a look at that dumbwaiter. I think it's an important clue."

We went to the kitchen together. Mary Anne looked around the room. "The dumbwaiter should be next to the pantry," she whispered. "I bet it's behind that painting."

It took two of us to lift the big painting off the wall. And sure enough, under the painting was a pair of wooden doors.

"Who's going to open them?" Mary Anne asked nervously.

"I'll do it," I volunteered. I put my hands on the metal handles.

"Mary Anne and I will stand guard and warn you if anyone comes," Kristy said. She stood near the door leading from the kitchen to the outside. Mary Anne watched at the door to the dining

173

room in case someone came in through the verandah.

"Be careful," Mary Anne told me. "Don't do anything dangerous."

"Here goes," I whispered to Claud as I slowly turned the handles and pulled the doors open.

We faced a large opening, with pulley ropes to our right and left. We leaned inside and looked up. "The shelves must be up there somewhere," Claud said. "Let's pull."

As I pulled on the rope we heard an awful squeaking noise. "That's one of the noises I've been hearing in my wall," I told Claud. Looking up, I could see the bottom of the dumbwaiter coming down towards us. "Whoever's trying to scare us has been pulling the dumbwaiter up and down to make that noise. . ."

Suddenly Claud screamed, "Watch out!"

Instinctively I ducked. Something jumped out of the dumbwaiter and sailed over my head.

"It's OK, Dawn," Claud said. "It was the cat."

Kristy jumped out of Spooky's way as he streaked past her and flew out of the kitchen. "How did he get in there?" she asked.

I pulled the rope to send the dumbwaiter up again. "I heard something fall down here when Spooky jumped out," I told Claud. We leaned into the space and looked down to the bottom of the shaft.

174

"I can see something," Claud said. I saw it too. It was the size of a paperback book, but that's all I could tell in the darkness. "It might be important," I told Claud. "I'm going to go in there and get it."

"No," Mary Anne said. "Dawn, don't." She wanted to pull me away from the dumbwaiter, but she wouldn't leave her post. "Please," she pleaded in a hoarse whisper.

"It's so dark down there," Claud said. "And what if someone comes?" She sounded as frightened as I was feeling.

I knew if I thought about it any longer I wouldn't do it, so I climbed in and dropped just over a metre down to the floor of the shaft. Above me I could see the bottom of the dumbwaiter shelves, and Claud peering anxiously down at me. The place gave me the creeps. I wished I had listened to Mary Anne. I couldn't wait to get out of there.

I bent over and picked up the object I'd seen. "It's a tape recorder," I called up to Claud.

"We should put it back in the dumbwaiter," she said. "We don't want to leave any evidence that we've been here."

I was feeling more claustrophobic by the second. "Hand me a chair," I told Claud, "so I can climb out."

Just then I heard Kristy hiss, "Listen, everyone! The Coopers are coming."

Dawn

Claud's face registered total panic. And I was *terrified* of being closed in that damp, dark hole but I still told Claud, "Shut the doors."

Claud whispered, "We'll come back as soon as we can," and closed me in.

I was in total darkness.

I heard the scraping noise of the painting being replaced on its hook. The next things I heard were footsteps above me and Elton Cooper cheerfully greeting my friends: "Good afternoon, girls. What are you all doing indoors on such a pretty day? . . . Oh, you aren't all here. One of you is missing."

"Dawn went into town," Kristy said quickly.

"Funny, we didn't pass her on the road," Elton said. My heartbeat was pounding in my ears.

"She hitched a lift," Claudia put in.

"And we're getting a snack," Kristy said. I heard the fridge door close. "Snacks for the hungry babysitters."

"Can we help you with anything?" Mary Anne asked. I could hear the tremor in her voice. Could Mr Cooper?

"You could bring the rest of the grocery bags in from the back of the car," he said.

I heard my friends hurry outside.

Oh, no. They were leaving me alone with the Coopers! What if the Coopers didn't leave the kitchen till after dinner? What if I had to stay in this dark, hot hole for hours and hours? What if I

176

ran out of oxygen and fainted—or worse? If they opened the dumbwaiter and found me, what would they do?

"Did you remember to buy the sausage for the meatballs?" I heard Elton ask.

A woman's voice answered, "You told me to, didn't you?"

"You shush, Maggie," Mr Cooper scolded. "Those girls will be right back."

I thought, *Maggie's a nickname for Margaret.* The hair rose on the back of my neck.

A minute later I heard the thumps of grocery bags being put on worktops and Kristy saying, "Mr and Mrs Cooper, you've been cooking us such lovely meals and everything. We want to do something for you for a change. So Mary Anne is going to serve you afternoon tea on the verandah while Claudia and I put the groceries away."

Please, I prayed. *Please say yes.*

Elton protested that it was their job to serve us tea. I held my breath. But at last he said, "Well, I was just thinking that Margaret could do with a break."

"And you'll take the break with her," Kristy insisted.

"Thank you," Elton said. "I will."

Thank you, Kristy. Thank you.

I heard the departing footsteps of the Coopers, then the sound of the painting being taken down. At last the doors of the dumbwaiter opened and I

Dawn

could see Claud's face above me. She handed me a chair. "Hurry," she whispered. I stood on the chair and climbed out of my prison. Claud leaned over and pulled up the chair. We quickly drew the shelves down and replaced the tape recorder on the middle shelf. "I bet if we played the tape we'd hear a woman's scream," Claud said.

When we'd raised the shelves again, we latched the dumbwaiter closed and put the painting back. Meanwhile, Mary Anne was practically having a heart attack, while Kristy made tea for the Coopers.

"Dawn, you'd better get out of here," Mary Anne whispered, "in case they come back."

Before I left the kitchen I told my fellow BSC detectives the most important thing I'd learned in the bottom of the dumbwaiter shaft: "Listen, everyone," I whispered. "Mrs Cooper can talk."

18th CHAPTER

Mary Anne

Thursday
7:30 p.m.

I don't have any ghosts on my suspects list. Just four LIVE suspects.

Suspect #1: The women with the European accent.

Evidence: Making inquiries about the Randolph mansion at the historical society.

Suspects #2 & #3: Margaret and Elton Cooper.

Evidence: Telling us and the kids scary stories. Lying to the

Mary Anne

Menderses. Pretending Mrs. Cooper can't speak.

Suspect #4: Georgio Irono.

Evidence: Has key to fourth floor and doesn't want us going up there. Thinks there's treasure in the attic.

If Georgio is our criminal, are the Coopers his partners in crime? Or is the woman with the accent his female accomplice? Or is Georgio the Coopers' accomplice?

"Thank you so much, Mary Anne," said Mr Cooper. "Doesn't that tea tray look splendid?"

I was walking across the veranda with a tray laden with tea, fruit cake and sliced peaches.

"Mrs Cooper thanks you too," Mr Cooper added. When Mrs Cooper flashed me a smile it gave me the creeps. I thought, she could thank me herself. She can speak.

"You're welcome," I said. I could hear my voice shaking. I put the tray down on the wicker coffee table in front of the Coopers.

Back in the kitchen, I told Claudia, "I think it's

time to ask the Tronos some more questions."
She agreed, and rang them to see if it was OK if
she dropped by for a visit and brought a friend.
Dinner was scheduled for eight o'clock. If we
hurried, we could spend half an hour with the
Tronos and be back before we were missed.
Kristy and Dawn said they'd stay behind to keep
an eye on the Coopers.

"Be careful," I warned them.

"You too," Kristy said.

I reminded her that the Tronos weren't
suspects.

"But their grandson is," Dawn replied. I saw
Claudia frown. She'd been spending a lot of time
with Georgio.

"We'll be careful," I told Kristy and Dawn. As
we hurried through the streets, I asked Claudia,
"What if Georgio's at his grandparents'?"

"He went into New Hampshire to buy some
special paint for the float. He won't be back for
ages."

The Tronos were just as sweet and nice as
Claudia had described them. We talked about
Founder's Day and enjoyed a glass of iced tea
before we peppered them with questions.

I began with, "Do you know the Coopers very
well?"

Mrs Trono looked at me quizzically and asked,
"The Coopers?"

"Margaret and Elton Cooper," Claudia said.

"The new caretakers at the Randolph estate."

"We met them once," Mrs Trono replied, "when we gave them our keys. Poor Mrs Cooper can't talk. I remember that."

"I always think of everybody knowing each other in a small town like Reese," I commented.

"But the Coopers aren't from Reese, dear," Mrs Trono said. "I've lived in Reese all my life. I would have known them if they were."

So the Coopers had lied to the Menderses about where they were from. I didn't want to alarm the Tronos, so I changed the subject.

"Was there a key to the third-floor staircase in the set of keys you gave the Coopers?" I asked.

"Certainly," Mr Trono answered. "I gave them a complete set. On my own keyring."

"I suppose a key could have fallen off," Claud suggested.

"Not from that keyring," Mrs Trono said. "It's a fine old thing. When you're a caretaker, your set of keys must be secure on their ring. You live by your keys."

"Georgio asked about our key to the third floor, too," Mrs Trono said. "Is everything all right at the mansion?"

I didn't want to worry these nice people. They'd have enough to worry about if Georgio was our culprit. So I said, "We've been doing some research on the mansion. About its history and everything."

182

"Like the story about Lydia Randolph," Claud added. She asked the Tronos if they'd heard the tragic tale of Lydia Randolph and George.

"Well," Mr Trono said when Claudia had finished the story, "I've never heard such an outlandish bit of nonsense in all my life. That sounds like the kind of silliness Millicent Ellsworth would come up with. It's probably in that book of hers."

Mrs Trono added, "You girls should know that the Randolph family have been outstanding citizens and benefactors of this town since its founding two hundred and fifty years ago. They loved their children and would want nothing but their happiness. They would never imprison their own daughter."

We left soon after that. As we were walking up the gravel driveway to the mansion, Claud asked me, "Do you think Georgio's trying to help us or scare us?"

"I think maybe he's been trying to help us," I said. Claudia smiled at that. "I think it's just the Coopers we have to be afraid of," I added. "I don't trust them one bit."

"Me neither," Claud said. "But I'm not afraid of Georgio any more. My gut feeling is that he's a good person. I really don't believe he'd want to do anything to frighten me—I mean us."

By then we'd reached the mansion. I went upstairs to tidy up for dinner and to write in our holiday notebook. Later, downstairs, I found dinner laid out buffet-style on the verandah. The children were happy but tired after the mini-fair and the beach outing with their parents. When we'd all sat down to eat, Mr Menders tapped his glass with a spoon and asked for our attention. He said if it was all right with the sitters, the adults would go to Boston the next day.

"But we'll be back tomorrow night," Mrs Menders added. "And we'll all spend Founders' Day together."

Mr Menders continued, "Our plan for the trip to Boston is to visit some wholesale suppliers of health foods." He looked at each of his children as he spoke their names. "Lionel. Jill. Jason. Martha. You should know that your mother and I are thinking very seriously of a permanent move to Reese. But, as I promised, I want to hear what each of you thinks about living here. So speak up."

Lionel spoke first. "I like it here better than I did at first."

"Me too," Jason said.

"How about you, Martha?" Mrs Menders asked.

Martha answered by asking, "Can Jody come for a sleepover some time?" Mr and Mrs Menders exchanged smiles. Martha was doing just fine.

"Can Dawn and her whole family come and

Mary Anne

live with us?" Jill asked. "We've got lots of room."

I pretended to cough into my napkin so Jill wouldn't see me laughing. I noticed that Kristy was doing the same thing.

"Well, I suppose it's just about settled then. We'll ask our lawyer to notify my cousin about our decision."

"I didn't know you *had* a cousin," Jason said. "How come we've never met him?"

"I haven't seen Charles Randolph myself since we were both about four years old," Mr Menders explained. "I remember my uncle saying years later that Charles had moved to Europe. Scotland, I think."

"Why do you have to let this cousin know whether we decide to live here?" Lionel asked.

"Because the will stipulates that I inherit this mansion only if we live here full-time," Mr Menders answered. "Otherwise, it goes to my cousin Charles."

"Dad, why didn't you tell us this before?" Lionel asked. "It's a pretty important detail."

I wondered the same thing.

"We didn't want to put that extra pressure on you," Mrs Menders explained. "This is a hard decision to make to begin with. We wanted to give you every advantage in adjusting to life here. If you were miserable we would turn down the offer of the estate and go on with our lives as we were.

185

Mary Anne

But as we see it, you're beginning to adjust very nicely."

All of the Menders kids admitted they liked Reese and living in the mansion, even Jill. I was glad—but I was also more than a little nervous about it.

Dawn whispered to me, "I've just remembered. Margaret Cooper spoke with an accent."

"From what country?" I whispered back.

Dawn answered by shrugging her shoulders.

After dinner, Lionel said he was going to the theatre, and asked if any of us wanted to go with him. We all said no. (He was doing fine on his own, and we had some sleuthing to do.) But I had an idea. "We'll walk you to the gate", I said, "if you'll play the accent game with us again."

I was hoping Dawn would recognize what country Mrs Cooper's accent was from by listening to Lionel's repertoire of accents.

"Only this time," I told Lionel as we escorted him down the drive, "let's see if you can say the same short sentence with each of the accents. That'll make it harder for you and for us. OK?"

"OK," he said. "I can do that."

Dawn had caught on. She told him to use the sentence, "You told me to, didn't you?"

Lionel began. We identified a French accent and a Swedish accent. Both times Dawn shook her head no, meaning that wasn't the way Mrs Cooper had spoken.

186

Then Lionel said, "Ye told me toe, didn't ye?"

Dawn asked him to say it again.

He did.

Dawn whispered, "That's it."

"So what country is it?" Lionel asked.

"Scotland—it's Scottish," Kristy said.

Lionel said she was right.

I felt a chill course through my body. Looking around at my friends, I could tell we were all thinking the same thing. If Mrs Cooper had a Scottish accent, then. . .

We said a quick goodbye to Lionel and raced back to the house. We practically ran up the stairs, and straight to my room. As soon as the door was closed, Dawn blurted out, "Elton Cooper must be Tom Menders' cousin!"

"And Margaret is his *Scottish* wife," I added.

"And they're trying to scare us—and the kids—because they want the mansion for themselves," Claud concluded.

"But we still have to prove it, you lot," Kristy said. "We need more evidence."

We decided that the next day we'd gather as much evidence as we could to prove our suspicions that Mr "Cooper" was really Charles Randolph. Then, when the Menderses got back from Boston we would tell them the whole story.

Mary Anne

That night I slept in Kristy's room again. When we heard footsteps on the top floor I was *more* frightened than I had been when I'd thought ghosts might be up there. Ghosts would be easier to deal with, I thought, than the deceitful Coopers. They wanted the mansion badly enough to come to America, impersonate caretakers, and do all the things they'd done to scare us and the kids. What else would they do? I wasn't sure I wanted to find out.

19th CHAPTER

Jessi

Today we found out
why so few clients
have been calling.
I hope you guys
aren't too disappointed
when you come
home and find
there aren't a lot of
baby - sitting jobs.

"What if we don't have any messages today either?" Mal asked. We were on our way to the Kishis' for our Friday BSC meeting.

I checked the machine the second we walked into Claud's room. No messages. I threw myself across the bed and moaned. "Mal, you know what this means, don't you? It means that we've ruined the reputation of the club. First the answering machine wasn't on for a whole twenty-four hours, and then we had to turn down jobs."

"Claud and the others are having a ball—no problems, no worries," Mal said. "Meanwhile, we've destroyed the club."

"When clients call today," I said, "let's apologize about the answering machine and be sure to tell them when the others will be back. And also tell them that if they've been disappointed by the club over the last week, it's our fault."

"That's a great idea," Mal said, "except for one thing."

"What?"

"You may have noticed that the phone isn't exactly ringing off the hook. No one's calling. They probably think it's hopeless. That there aren't any sitters."

"Then maybe we should phone them and explain everything," I suggested.

"OK," Mal agreed. "Who shall we call first?"

190

"The clients we know the best," I said. "I'll start by calling the Braddocks."

My stomach was doing cartwheels as I punched in the telephone number for the Braddocks. Mrs Braddock answered. "Hi, Mrs Braddock," I said. "This is Jessi Ramsey."

Mrs Braddock asked me how I was. I said fine and asked her how *she* was.

"I'm just running out of the door," she said. "Everyone's packed into the van. We're going on a two-week camping trip."

"Have a wonderful time," I told her.

"What was it you wanted, Jessi?"

"Oh, nothing, really," I said. "Just letting you know that the Babysitters Club will be here for you when you come back. Call any time. You can always leave a message on the BSC machine. 'Bye."

I rang off and told Mal, "The Braddocks haven't called because they don't need sitters. They're going on holiday." I handed her the phone. "I'll make a note about their schedule in the record book while you make the next call."

She punched in the Perkinses' phone number, listened for a while and rang off without speaking. "A machine answered," she explained. "It said, 'You've reached the Perkins residence. We're on holiday till July the thirtieth. Messages for Bill Murphy can be left with this machine.' As I didn't have a message for Bill Murphy," Mal continued, "I rang off."

"So the Braddocks and Perkinses haven't called for sitters because they're going on holiday," I said. "That's a relief." I was relieved enough to notice that I was hungry. "Let's find something to eat before we make any more calls."

We found a bag of fruit gums under Claud's bed. Mal ripped them open and we dug in. Two green and one red fruit gum later, I rang the Arnolds and learned that Marilyn and Carolyn had gone to visit their grandmother for a week.

"We'll be calling for sitters as soon as they're back," Mrs Arnold told me. "Hope you're all having a wonderful holiday."

Next Mal called the Addisons. When she'd rung off she told me, "Corrie and Sean are away at holiday camp."

"This is great," I said. "People aren't phoning because they don't *need* sitters, not because they don't want the BSC any more. It makes sense."

"It does," Mal said as she stuffed a green fruit gum into her mouth. I couldn't understand what she said next because of the way the sweets stuck to her teeth.

"What did you say?" I asked.

She chewed and swallowed. "I said, 'I'm still hungry.'"

We both thought that was hilarious. We searched Claud's room for a snack that was a little

Jessi

more nourishing than sweets, and we couldn't stop giggling.

At last we found a bag of corn crisps. While we ate, we talked about how much fun the Reese contingent must be having and how we wished *we* were hanging around in a seaside town without a care in the world.

"The only fun thing happening here," I said, "is Celebrate America! Day, and we have to work then."

"And work hard," Mal added. "Do you realize that between us we'll be looking after fifteen kids?"

"Maybe we should join forces and do some kind of activity with all of them," I suggested.

"But they're different ages, Jessi. What kind of activity can we do with kids ranging in age from two to ten?" Mal asked.

"What do two-year-olds and ten-year-olds have in common?" I replied.

"Absolutely nothing."

"Kristy wouldn't let that hold her back," I said. "And neither would the others. They love challenges."

"You're right." I took the last red fruit gum out of the bag.

"Then let's come up with something wonderful to do with all the kids," she said.

I rolled the fruit gum across the BSC notebook to Mal. "If someone invented the wheel," I said,

193

Jessi

"then we can work out what to do with fifteen kids."

"Inventing the wheel might have been easier," Mal commented as she rolled the fruit gum back to me. I didn't know then that the idea we were looking for was in that round fruit gum.

20th CHAPTER

Kristy

Friday
9:00 p.m.

I am writing this by candlelight. A terrible thunderstorm is raging. The electricity and phones are out. We're alone with six children — and two evil adults. Above all else, we must protect the children.

"Kristy, having all you sitters here this week is working out even better than I'd hoped," Lisa said. "You're doing a terrific job."

It was just after breakfast on Friday, and the adults were getting ready to leave for Boston. I wondered if I should tell Lisa about the Coopers. I decided against it. We needed more proof. It would be incredibly embarrassing if we accused the Coopers, only to find out we'd been wrong. Besides, what were we accusing them of? Telling us scary stories? Making noises in the wall? Saying someone was mute when she wasn't? Being Scottish? We needed more evidence.

But first, I reminded myself, we had baby-sitting responsibilities. Dawn and I had cooked up an idea for persuading Jill to join the swimming team. When the adults had left for Boston we took her aside.

"Kristy and I have been talking about you, Jill," Dawn began. "Now that it looks as though you'll be moving to Reese, we thought you might like to start a babysitting club of your own."

Jill's eyes widened with interest.

"We can explain how we run our club and answer all your questions about babysitting," I added.

"I've got a question already," Jill said. "How did you learn how to babysit?" I held back a grin. Jill had asked the perfect question.

"By sitting for our own sisters and brothers,"

196

Dawn answered. "You know—the way Kristy sits for Karen and Andrew."

"Lionel's too big for me to babysit for," Jill said. "And Jason wouldn't let me."

"What about Martha?" I asked.

"She'd say I was treating her like a baby."

"You could babysit for Martha without telling her," Dawn explained. "Sometimes I do that with my brother, Jeff. When we're doing water sports, like sailing, I watch out for him. I've worked in a lot of babysitting practice that way."

"Hey, I know! If you and Martha were both on the swimming team," I suggested, "you could watch Martha and have fun too."

"Dawn has fun with me," Jill said happily. "And I'm younger than her."

"That's right," Dawn replied. "Now you understand an important idea about babysitting. You can have *fun* with the kids you sit for, even when they're your own brothers or sisters."

Just then Martha came out to the verandah for our what-are-we-going-to-do-today meeting and asked, "Dawn, what are we going to do today?"

"Martha, how'd you like to join the swimming team?" Jill asked.

"I'm not joining unless you do," Martha muttered.

"But I'm going to," Jill told her. "We're both going to."

Martha smiled widely. "Goody!" she said. "Goody, goody and triple goody!"

After our meeting, Lionel and Jason went off to the ballfield, saying they'd catch up with us at dinnertime. Claudia was spending the morning working on our Founders' Day float. Dawn was taking the Menders sisters to the pool. Mary Anne and I went into town with Andrew and Karen.

Our first stop was the photocopying shop. Claud had asked us to make four copies of a picture from one of the old Randolph family albums. It was the photo of the man who had looked so mysteriously familiar to her. When we'd left the copy shop, Mary Anne took us to the historical society. The door was open, so we walked in.

"Hi, Mrs Butterfield," Mary Anne said to the woman at the front desk. While I distracted Karen and Andrew with a painting of a boat in a storm, I strained to hear Mary Anne's conversation with Mrs Butterfield.

"I dropped by to ask you a question about the woman you told me wanted to know about the Randolph estate," Mary Anne was saying. "You said she had a heavy accent. Do you remember if it was a Scottish accent?"

"Yes, it could have been Scottish," Mrs Butterfield replied. "But why don't you ask her yourself? She's here now." She pointed to the library. We looked in that direction. But no one was there. "She must have gone out the back way," Mrs Butterfield explained.

I ran through the library to the side window. Sure enough, Margaret Cooper was hurrying down the street. Mrs Butterfield appeared beside me. "There she is," she said. "It's too bad she left without meeting you. She was *so* interested in knowing who else was making inquiries about the Randolph Mansion." Ah-ha! So Margaret knew about us now. I was afraid of what she would do next.

When we were outside again Mary Anne and I decided that we should go back to the estate straight away. We needed to warn Claud that Margaret knew Mary Anne had been doing research on the Randolph estate. And that we knew she could speak! I promised Karen and Andrew that when we got back to the mansion they could watch a video. So far we'd been able to steer the kids out of the scary situation and I intended to keep it that way.

Later, while Mary Anne organized a video for the kids, I went out to the shed, where Claud was supposed to be working on the props for the float. She wasn't there. I looked in the gardens for Georgio. He wasn't there.

When I reported back to Mary Anne she said, "Maybe they're upstairs."

"Claud told me she might hunt for clothes in

Kristy

the attic this morning," I said. "Come on."

The door to the third-floor staircase was unlocked.

"What if Mr Cooper's up there?" Mary Anne whispered.

A cold, clammy feeling washed over me. We crept silently up the stairs. The first thing I noticed on the third floor was that the attic door was closed. The second thing I noticed was that the door to Lydia's room was open.

I signalled Mary Anne to stay where she was while I investigated. The closer I inched to that open door the more frightened I became. What would I see? What if whoever was in there saw *me*? The image of a white-haired woman answering to the name of Lydia flashed through my mind.

I held my breath and peered into the room. Two figures—male and female—were bending over a wicker basket.

I gasped.

And Claudia and Georgio screamed, which made me scream. But Mary Anne screamed the loudest of all.

When we had calmed down, Georgio locked the door to Lydia's room and the four of us went to my room to talk. Mary Anne and I sat on my bed. Georgio and Claudia sat on the window seat. "Georgio knows everything and he's totally

200

innocent," Claudia told us. "He's been suspicious of the Coopers himself."

"Something's bothered me about those two from the beginning," Georgio explained. "Even before you came here. When I realized they were trying to scare you lot, and they claimed not to have a key to the third floor, I got really suspicious."

"What about the treasure in the attic?" Mary Anne said.

"I thought that somehow the Coopers had heard about what Mr Randolph said when he was dying, and then took the caretakers' job to try to find this so-called treasure for themselves. Now I know they want the whole place."

"So you've been hanging around us because you were suspicious of the Coopers?" I asked.

"That's the second reason," Georgio said. He smiled at Claud. "The first reason I've been hanging around you is because of Claudia."

Claud looked shyly at the floor before saying, "Anyway, Georgio's got a key to the third-floor bedroom we've been calling Lydia's room. So we went up there. We'd just worked out how the light has been going off and on when Kristy scared us."

"Sorry about that," I said. "Tell us about the light."

"The lamp is connected to a timer," Georgio

explained. "The kind people use to make burglars think someone's at home."

"In this case the burglars themselves are using it," I commented.

"They hid the timer in an old sewing basket," Claud continued. "We left it there so they won't know that we're on to them."

"They might already know," Mary Anne said softly. "At least, Margaret might." She told Claud and Georgio about Mrs Cooper and the historical society.

"By the way," Claud told us, "before the Coopers left this morning, Elton reminded me that it's their day off. He said he and Mrs Cooper wouldn't be back till this evening."

"Good," I said. "That gives us plenty of time to hunt for more evidence."

"Let's check their rooms," Claud suggested.

"Isn't that an invasion of privacy?" I wondered out loud.

"Look at all the creepy things they've been doing to us," Claud reminded me.

I thought about the kids. I was convinced that the Coopers were a threat to their safety.

"How are we going to get into those rooms?" I asked.

"I've got a master key that should fit the lock," Georgio said. "While you're up there I'll weed the back garden. That way I can warn you if I see them coming back here."

"How will you warn us?" I asked.

"Their bedroom window faces the back garden," Georgio said. "So look out every couple of minutes. I'll take off my hat if I see them."

We heard footsteps then, and stopped talking about the Coopers. Then we heard children's voices singing the theme song from *The Little Mermaid*. Karen and Martha bounced into the room. Martha, her hair still wet from swimming, announced, "I'm in the swimming team. So's Jill."

We all congratulated Martha and promised to go to the girls' first swimming meeting on Monday.

After lunch, Mary Anne said she'd keep an eye on the girls and Anrew while the rest of us explored the Coopers' rooms. "Are you coming, Claud?" I asked.

"I've got to do something else," Claud answered in a vague, distracted voice. I thought maybe she'd drift off and spend the afternoon mooning over Georgio. But Georgio wasn't the man she had on her mind. "Did you two photocopy that picture?" she asked.

When I'd given her the copies, she said she'd be in the dining room if we needed her.

Dawn and I took the back stairs to the Coopers' private quarters. As I turned Georgio's key in the lock I told Dawn, "I hate sneaking around like this."

"I love it," Dawn confessed. "And they deserve it!"

The door opened into a sitting room. It had no windows. "Let's start in the bedroom," I suggested.

Dawn began her search with the wardrobe while I peered out of the bedroom window. I looked down at the garden and saw Georgio, in a straw hat, weeding with a hoe.

"There isn't much in here," Dawn said. "It's as if they haven't even unpacked." Then in a trembling voice she added, "Kristy, look." I turned away from the window and saw that Dawn was holding up a floor-length white satin gown. "It was in the back of the wardrobe," she explained. "It must be the dress that's missing from the armoire in the attic."

"And I bet you anything that's the dress that the ghost of Mary Randolph wears on the widow's walk," I added.

"I saw a desk in the other room," Dawn said. "I'm going to search it." While I kept an eye on Georgio and his hat I noticed that the sky was darkening. It looked as though a big storm were heading our way.

"Kristy," Dawn called, "come here." I ran into the sitting room. Dawn was huddled over the desk. "You have to see this," she whispered. She pointed to a page in a notebook:

Ten - Step Plan for when company leaves:
 1. poison ivy oil on inside of Lionel's
    and Mrs. Menders' clothes
 2. get Georgio fired for fooling around
    with sitter
 3. plumbing breakdown
 4. disappearance of Jason's baseball
    glove (and any replacements)
 5. small electrical fire in Martha's
    bedroom

Fire? These are evil people, I thought. They'll even hurt children to get what they want.

"I expect they're waiting till we leave to get serious," Dawn said. "And that's only half the list. Steps six to ten aren't here."

"Well, this is all the evidence we need," I told Dawn. "It *proves* that the Coopers are up to no good."

"And that Georgio's innocent," Dawn added. I had to agree with her.

Just then I thought I heard a car on the drive. I ran to the other room and looked out of the window. Georgio's hat was on the ground next to him. "Hurry!" I called to Dawn. "They're back."

We shoved the list into the drawer where Dawn had found it, locked the door to the rooms, and ran down the stairs. Margaret came into the

205

kitchen from outside a split second after we entered from the back stairs. Had she seen us coming from her rooms? She smiled at me but her eyes were cold and calculating.

We later learned that while we were investigating the Coopers' quarters, Claudia was coming up with another piece of evidence incriminating the Coopers. She had gone to the dining room to experiment with the photocopies we'd made for her. She wanted to work out why the man in the photo seemed familiar to her. She'd thought that the man reminded her of a woman she knew. To check that idea Claud drew wavy shoulder-length hair on the photocopy. Then she added eye-shadow and lipstick. The resulting image didn't remind her of anyone she knew. Looking at the hair she'd drawn on this female version of Mr Randolph's ancestor gave Claudia another idea.

She began with a fresh photocopy. This time she added a beard and moustache. It still wasn't what she was looking for, but she felt that she was coming closer. She pulled out another copy. This time she added a more delicate moustache and a smaller beard. When she finished, Elton Cooper was looking at her from the doctored photocopy.

At that moment a clap of thunder startled Claud. She was even more startled when the thunder was followed by a male voice anouncing, "Big storm coming. Stay away from the windows." Claud looked up and gasped. Elton

Cooper was standing in front of her. She clapped her hand over the image that looked so much like him and said, "Thank you, I will." Then she gathered up her papers and clutched them to her chest. "I'll check the kids." Hurrying from the room, she wondered if he had seen what she was doing.

Dawn

Friday
11 p.m.

I almost wish I still thought this house was haunted. It would probably be really spooky to be here in this fierce storm with the electricity out, wondering whether a restless spirit was roaming the halls. But it wouldn't be as bad as knowing that a pair of calculating criminals is in the house with us. I've never been so scared in my life.

Dawn

Everyone except me has fallen asleep. I can't help thinking about that dreadful story Elton told us. What will the Coopers do next to try to frighten us and the children? I'm going to stay awake for as long as I can and keep watch over everyone.

Will the morning ever come?

"Dawn, Dawn—where are you?"

Jill ran into the kitchen and threw her arms around me.

"What's wrong?" I asked. "What is it?"

"I'm scared," she said.

Another clap of thunder rattled the air. I felt Jill shudder. "It's only a storm," I told her. "You're safe inside with us. Come on, we'll find the others."

Within minutes, the late summer afternoon became so dark that we had to turn on the parlour lights. And because the storm was so violent and close, we unplugged the TV and VCR. Then we tried to start up a game of Junior Pictionary, but the kids were distracted by the crashes of thunder and bolts of lightning, and by the window-rattling winds and torrential rains.

"What about Lionel and Jason?" Martha asked. "They'll get wet."

"They'll get *very* wet," Karen added. "Completely soaked."

"They'll be all right," I assured the girls. But I felt more worried than I let on. I hoped Lionel knew that they shouldn't walk home from the softball field during a lightning storm.

At last the girls and Andrew started paying attention to Pictionary. Kristy took Mary Anne and Claudia out to the hall to tell them what we'd found in the Cooper's rooms. A few minutes later Mary Anne and Kristy came back and Kristy whispered to me, "Claud's got something to show you."

In the hall, Claud handed me a picture. I looked at it and asked, "Where did you find this drawing of Elton? Is it from a *wanted* poster?" I was more afraid of Elton than ever. "Is he wanted by the FBI?"

Claud explained that what I was looking at wasn't Elton Cooper, but one of the Randolph ancestors. The evidence was mounting that Elton Cooper really was Charles Randolph, Mr Menders' cousin.

"While you were with the kids just now," Claud told me, "we made three rules to follow till we can tell the Menderses about the Coopers.

210

One, don't go anywhere alone in the mansion. Two, don't leave any of the children alone—even for an instant. Three, don't act suspicious of the Coopers'. We don't want them to know how much we know about them."

I agreed to obey the rules, then asked, "What time did the Menderses say they'd be back?"

"After dinner," Claud reminded me.

"Maybe they'll come early," I said hopefully, "because of the storm."

A clap of thunder preceded a crackling flash of lightning. Then the lights went out. Claud and I rushed back into the parlour to help Kristy calm the kids down.

"It's dark," Andrew said. "Is it night, Kristy? Do I have to go to bed? I'm not tired."

While Kristy explained to Andrew that even though it was dark it wasn't night, Claud and I told the girls that we were going to have a great adventure. "We'll pretend this is long ago, before people had electricity," Mary Anne said.

"Just like the characters we're going to play on the float," I added.

"Goody!" Karen said. "Let's find some torches and pretend they're candles."

Claud and I left Kristy and Mary Anne with the kids while we searched for torches. "I wish Lionel and Jason were back," I told Claud as we made our way down the darkened corridor. At that instant a zigzag of lightning illuminated the figure of Margaret Cooper. She was tiptoeing toward us, carrying an unlit torch. Claud and I were so startled we didn't say anything at first.

Margaret silently turned the torch on and handed it to us. In that dull yellow light it was hard to tell if she was smiling or sneering.

We thanked her and went back to the parlour to give the torch to Kristy. Then we made our way to the kitchen to put together a snack for the kids as best we could in the darkened house. We were spreading peanut butter on crackers when we heard a knock on the outside kitchen door. I was expecting Lionel and Jason, but it was Georgio. A powerful gust of wind came into the room with him.

"Is everyone OK?" he asked.

Georgio was dressed in yellow raingear and high, black rubber fireman's boots. As we talked he pulled out of his pockets three torches, a bundle of storm candles and a transistor radio.

"Do you think the kids' parents will be able to drive home in this storm?" Claud asked.

"I had hoped they were already back," Georgio said. "I doubt they can drive from Boston in this weather," he told us. "The safest thing for them to do would be to stay in Boston till it's over."

Elton came into the kitchen while Georgio was telling us that the storm was going to last for several hours and could cause local flooding.

212

"You're on high ground so there's no danger of flooding up here," Georgio explained. He added that as an auxiliary volunteer fireman, he'd be keeping an eye on flood levels and checking that the residents of Reese were safe.

We told Georgio that Lionel and Jason hadn't come back. "I'll go and look for them," he said. "And I'll check on you and the kids again as soon as I can."

"You don't need to worry about them," Elton said. "They're safe with Margaret and me."

Huh! I thought.

Before Georgio left, he squeezed Claud's hand and gave her a quick kiss on the cheek. "Be careful, Claudia," he warned. Then he opened the door and went back out into the storm.

I wondered if Elton was thinking he could use that kiss as evidence that Georgio was "fooling around with a sitter".

For the next hour we kept the children busy with games and singing. We all felt a bit better when Lionel and Jason got back. Georgio, true to his word, had gone to the playground to look for them, and found them in the rec barn with a few other kids. He had taken all the kids home, then gone out into the storm again to help more stranded people. Claud was very proud of him.

Kristy and Mary Anne made sure to tell the Coopers that since it was their day off, we could manage our own dinner. When the Coopers protested, saying this was an emergency, Kristy told them that making dinner by candlelight would be a fun, distracting activity for our charges. But the real reason we'd decided to make dinner ourselves was that we simply didn't trust the Coopers. What if they tried to poison us or something?

We tried to keep our spirits up while we put together a cold supper of salads and sandwiches. Lionel was a terrific sport and told the kids funny stories. Every once in a while we'd turn on the transistor radio and listen to the emergency storm reports. Each report included a warning to stay at home and not to drive. I was pretty sure that the adults wouldn't be home that night.

"I'm cold," Karen complained.

"Me, too," Jill added.

They were right. The temperature was dropping. Kristy and Mary Anne went off to find sweaters and sweatshirts for everyone while the rest of us cleared up the kitchen.

While we were working, Margaret and Elton Cooper came into the kitchen from upstairs. "It's getting nippy," Elton said. "I'm going to make a fire in the parlour. You all come in there as soon as you've finished in here." Had he been spying on us? And wasn't there something about fire on the list the Coopers had made?

Half an hour later we were warming ourselves in front of a wood fire in the big front parlour.

"Let's tell scary stories," Jason said.

I didn't think that was a very good idea, but Karen and the others did, and Mr Cooper jumped at the opportunity.

"I know a true story," he said. "It's about the people who used to live in this house."

He then told the story of Reginald and Mary Randolph—the one we'd read in Millicent Ellsworth's so-called history of Reese. But he added another episode that even Millicent wouldn't have had the nerve to invent.

"In 1879, twenty years after Reginald's boat sank," Elton said, "a fishing vessel from Reese called *First Catch* was out at sea when a sudden summer storm threatened the lives of all on board."

Elton told his story with dramatic touches worthy of Lionel, but this was the basic plot. As the boat, *First Catch*, was being dangerously tossed by the waves, another boat, apparently untroubled by the storm, appeared next to it. The second boat led *First Catch* and its crew safely to shore. But instead of seeking safe harbour itself, the beacon boat headed back to sea.

In a flash of lightning, the Captain of *First Catch* saw the name of the other boat painted on its side: *Mary*. The captain knew that *Mary* was the name of Reginald Randolph's vessel, the one that had sunk twenty years earlier. He realized that what he'd suspected during their miraculous rescue was true. He and his crew had been saved by a ghost ship with a ghost crew. In his last glimpse of the phantom ship, the captain of *First Catch* saw a woman standing next to the captain. The woman was dressed in white.

The next morning the captain of *First Catch* learned that Mary Randolph had perished the night before, "hurled to her death by the violent winds of the storm" (as Elton put it), on the very night that the phantom ship saved the captain and his crew.

While Elton was telling the story, Margaret left the room. I wondered what mischief—or worse—she was up to. Would we soon hear screams and creaking noises? Would a ghostly vision in white pass the open parlour door? Just as Elton finished, Margaret returned carrying a tray with cups of hot chocolate.

There was a hush in the room. The children seemed frightened by Elton's story. And the babysitters were afraid of the Coopers.

Karen broke the silence. "Oh, goody!" she exclaimed. "Hot chocolate. I love it."

Margaret smiled what I used to think of as her "pretty smile". Now I thought of it as her "fake smile". What if she'd put poison in that hot chocolate? I jumped up and took the tray from her. "I'll serve it," I offered. "And you sit down, Margaret. It's your day off, remember?"

Clever Claud understood what I was doing and

why. She stood up, too. "I'll help," she said as she handed the first cup of hot chocolate to Margaret. "Could you tell us if it's cooled off enough for the children to drink?"

Margaret took a sip of the cocoa, smiled, and made the OK sign. Now that Margaret had had some, we served the others.

"What splendid babysitters you girls are," Elton said. "Worrying about the cocoa being too hot. You think of everything."

Was he on to us?

When the children had finished their cocoa we wished the Coopers goodnight, though I, for one, didn't mean it. Jill took my hand as we climbed the stairs. "Dawn, I'm scared," she whispered. I noticed that Jason was staying as close as possible to his big brother and each of the other kids was holding a sitter's hand. We had no trouble persuading the kids that it was the perfect night for a "sleepover party" in Kristy and Mary Anne's rooms.

But before settling down for the night we all sat around in Kristy's room to talk. We wanted to make sure the children understood that the story Elton told them was make-believe. Lionel was a big help. He demonstrated how Elton had changed his voice and used pauses to make the story scarier.

"But I *saw* the lady in white," Jill whispered fearfully.

217

Dawn

"When?" I asked.

"Last night. Spooky jumped on my bed and woke me up. I wanted him to sleep on my bed, but he ran away. I tried to catch him. That's when I saw her. I thought it was Claudia or Mary Anne practising for the parade. But the lady didn't turn around when I said your names."

I knew who "the lady in white" was, but I was determined not to tell the kids that the Coopers were trying to scare them. However, I didn't want them worrying about ghosts either. I didn't know what to say.

All the kids were listening to Jill. "Then the lady in white opened the door and went upstairs to the attic."

"Was it a ghost?" Karen asked.

"I think so," Jill said.

"I don't like ghosts," said Martha.

"It wasn't a ghost," Kristy said firmly. "It was Mrs Cooper in her nightgown or something. Maybe she was checking on us."

"It wasn't a nightgown," Jill said. "It was a fancy dress, like the ones in the attic."

"I bet it was Mary Randolph's ghost," said Jason.

"I'm sure it was Mrs Cooper, Jill," I said. "She must have a very fancy nightgown. Maybe even an antique one. There's nothing to be afraid of."

"Well, I'm scared anyway," Jill said. "I hate

218

it here. I want to go back to Boston."

"Me, too," Martha said.

I looked around at my friends. How would we ever calm these kids' fears? How would we calm our own? I couldn't wait for morning to come.

Mallory

Our baby-sitting charges had a great time on Celebrate America! Day. They were all in the parade.

Claud, thanks for saying we could eat anything we could find in your room. We ate a bag of blue corn chips and a bag of fruit gums.

"Jessi!" I shouted into the phone a couple of hours after our Friday meeting, "I've had a great idea. I know what we can do with the kids we're sitting for on Celebrate America! Day." I realized that Jessi was probably holding the phone about a metre away from her ear by then. I lowered my voice. "We can be the 'BSC on Wheels' and decorate the kids and their wheels in red, white and blue. Those round fruit gums inspired me."

"You mean the kids will ride bikes?" Jessi asked.

"Not just bikes," I said. "Whatever they want that's on wheels. Skateboards, roller blades, tricycle, anything. And we'll make a sign."

Jessi loved my idea. We spent for ever on the phone making plans. When we rang off we both had a lot of kids to talk to—fifteen to be exact.

I started with my brothers and sisters by making "BSC on Wheels" the subject of conversation at dinner.

Adam, Byron and Jordon wanted to skateboard in the parade. As you can't do much to decorate a skateboard they promised that first thing next morning, which was Celebrate America! Day, they'd help Vanessa, Nicky, Margo and Claire decorate their bikes.

My dad said as he was going to the parade anyway, he'd be an extra sitter and help out, especially during the parade. Good old Dad.

221

Mallory

After dinner I helped my brothers and sisters sort out red, white and blue clothes. I lent Vanessa my favourite T-shirt, which is red and white striped, with blue stars around the neck and sleeves. Adam said he'd wear a red baseball cap, Byron could wear a white one, and Jordan, blue.

Then I phoned the Rodowskys. Mrs Rodowsky thought it was a great idea for us to "roll" together in the parade. But I knew it was more important that the Rowdowsky kids like the plan. So I asked to speak to each of them, starting with Jackie.

"Great!" Jackie the walking disaster said when he heard the idea. "I haven't had an accident in a long time. And my bike's not broken any more." I decided to ask my dad to keep an extra close watch on Jackie, the *rolling* disaster.

Shea, who's nine, said he'd be in the parade if the triplets would. When he found out that they were going to be skateboarding, he was triple excited, because he skateboards too. Archie, who's only four, didn't quite follow what I was talking about, but his mother understood and said he could ride his tricycle in the parade. She also said she'd help the boys decorate their wheels first thing in the morning and give us an extra hand during the day if we needed it.

Meanwhile, Jessi went to the Braddocks' house. She invited Becca to go along with her.

"Can we Rollerblade there?" Becca asked. "You can teach me on the way."

"I don't want to start by teaching you on the street," Jessi told her sister. "Anyhow, we have to be back home before it gets dark. We should bike to the Braddocks' and back."

Becca is good friends with Haley Braddock, so she went with Jessi, even though she was angry about not being able to Rollerblade. And she sulked all the way.

Seven-year-old Matt Braddock is deaf, which is why Jessi didn't just call the Braddocks on the phone. She could have called and talked to Haley and Mrs Braddock, but she wanted to discuss "BSC on Wheels" with Matt, too. Matt communicates with American Sign Language (ASL), and Jessi's good at signing. (The rest of us sitters have learned some ASL too, but Jessi's the best.) When she signed to Matt about our idea for the parade, he signed back: "Good idea. I'll Rollerblade. I can wear blue jean shorts and a white shirt with a red sweatband around my head. Is that OK?"

Jessi signed, "It's better than OK. It's perfect!"

Haley liked the idea, too. She said (so Becca could understand) and signed (for her brother), "I think being in the parade will be a lot of fun, too. I'll ride on my skateboard and wear red tights and a big white T-shirt with a blue sash."

223

Mallory
ﾂ

Biking home, Jessi was pleased with how well her visit to the Braddocks had gone. But she wasn't pleased with Becca, who continued to complain about not being able to Rollerblade in the parade.

"You can ride your bike," Jessi said.

"Haley's not riding her bike," Becca shot back. "She's skateboarding."

Jessi reminded Becca that Vanessa Pike would be on a bike. But Becca wasn't listening (or was pretending not to listen). She pulled ahead on her bike and stayed about half a block ahead of Jessi all the way home.

Back at home, Jessi didn't even have time to talk to Becca, much less give her a Rollerblading lesson. She had to phone the Marshalls. They were going to be Jessi's biggest babysitting responsibility during Celebrate America!

Nina is four and Eleanor is only two years old—young enough to require *constant* supervision. Nina could ride her two-wheeler with stabilizers. But Jessi realized she'd have to push Eleanor in her buggy. She made a mental note to dress in red, white and blue herself.

Mrs Marshall liked the plan. "But I won't have time to decorate Nina's bike and the buggy," she told Jessi.

"That's all right," Jessi said. "I'll get some crêpe paper and streamers before I come over in the morning."

224

"I've got about a dozen American flags left over from a Fourth of July party," Mrs Marshall offered. "You could use those."

When Jessi had phoned and told me this, I phoned Logan and asked him if he could help us during Celebrate America! At first he sounded grumpy, as if he didn't want to talk to me about *anything*. But when I told him we were putting the kids in the parade, Logan sounded friendlier. In the end, he came round and said he'd help us. As my dad was going to work with me, I asked Logan to call Jessi and see what he could do to help her.

When Jessi and I talked on the phone later, she told me that Logan was going to pick up the Braddock kids (and that Becca was going with them instead of her).

We decided to meet in front of the town hall. I spent the next two hours making our signs. It was *very* late when I eventually got to bed.

The next morning my group was the first one at the town hall. I saw Kristy's brother Sam riding his unicycle around the town green and beckoned to him.

"I don't know how I did it," I told Jessi when she and her group arrived a few minutes later, "but somehow I persuaded Sam to let me decorate his unicycle with red, white and blue crêpe paper. And to carry our leading banner."

When I looked around at our fifteen kids, it was

225

hard to believe we'd been so nervous about Celebrate America! All the kids were sticking together and happy about the parade.

And Mr Braddock videotaped us, which was great because I wanted Kristy to see how Sam looked. He held our banner up high as he wove down the street on his unicycle. The sign read:

BSC KIDS ON WHEELS

The banners at the back of our group were pinned to Vanessa's and Becca's shirts. They said:

KEEP THE GOOD TIMES ROLLING

After the parade, everyone went over to the ballfield for an all-American picnic and some games. The fire department had set up a big barbecue pit and were selling hot dogs (very American) and grilled chicken. There was also potato salad, fizzy drinks, apple pie and ice cream. What a feast! We put two big picnic tables together for our group and stuck our signs in between them.

After lunch the kids took part in the games and arts-and-crafts activities. The highlights of the afternoon included Jackie Rodowsky winning the sack race and Matt coming in first in an egg-and-spoon race.

But the highlight of the highlights was that so

226

many people sought out Jessi and me to say thank you to the BSC. They weren't just saying thank you for being in the Celebrate America! parade, but for all the good work the BSC does. Even my mother congratulated us, and thanked me for looking after my brothers and sisters so she could work in the make-your-own-kite booth.

That night Jessi and I held a mini-BSC sleepover at her house. We just relaxed and celebrated!

23rd CHAPTER

Claudia

Saterday
11:30 p.m.

Wat a day! Wat a nikt! I'll never forgit it as long as I live.

Thanks evrybody for all the help with the floot. Sory if I scard you with my costum.

"Today's the parade, today's the parade!" Andrew chanted.

"Andrew, you've just trodden on me," complained Karen.

I opened my eyes and looked around. Karen, Jill, Martha, Dawn, Kristy and I had slept on the floor in Mary Anne's room. Andrew was trying, unsuccessfully, to walk between us. He plopped down on my stomach. "Is my mummy home yet?" he asked.

"I don't know," I said. I shifted him off me so I could get up and look out of the window. The only signs of the storm were a couple of broken tree limbs. It was a clear, sunshiny day, perfect for a Founders' Day parade and carnival. But first, I remembered with a shudder, we had to deal with the Coopers—who weren't even really the Coopers. And we couldn't do that until Mr and Mrs Menders came home.

I was thinking about the complicated story we had to tell the Menderses when I saw their estate car pull into the drive. "They're here!" I shouted to the others.

We ran down the stairs and out of the front door to greet them, and the Engles.

"Well, well!" Mrs Menders exclaimed. "I've never in my life had such a greeting!"

There was a lot of hugging and kissing and talking about the storm. Then we went into the house for breakfast.

Lionel and Jason announced that they were going to play softball but would be home for lunch and the parade. Before they left, Lionel whispered to me that they wouldn't be part of our float. "We've got other plans," he said mysteriously.

Then Jill told her parents that she and Martha were going to a swimming team practice, and that they didn't need a babysitter. "I can keep an eye on Martha," she explained.

When Kristy was absolutely sure that neither of the Coopers were around, she asked Mr and Mrs Menders if we could have a private meeting with them in the front parlour.

When we were all seated, Kristy used her most businesslike tone to start the meeting. "This will come as a shock to you," she began, "but we have evidence that the Coopers aren't who they say they are."

Over the next half an hour we laid out all that we'd learned about the Coopers.

We described how they'd tried to convince us and the children that the mansion was haunted.

Kristy told them about what the Coopers planned to do to make life in the mansion miserable—and dangerous—for everyone.

I showed them the photo of their Randolph ancestor and my photocopy of it with the added beard and moustache.

Dawn reported that not only had she heard

"Mrs Cooper" *speak*, but that the woman had a Scottish accent. "So the reason she pretended she couldn't speak," I added, "was because she didn't want anyone to know she was from Scotland."

"Where are the Coop—I mean the Randolphs—now?" Mrs Menders asked. She looked worried.

"They said they were going to buy groceries," Mary Anne answered.

"Well, that gives us some time to decide how to handle this situation," Mr Menders said. He looked grim and determined.

"You girls were right not to let on to the Coopers that you suspected them," Mrs Menders added. "Keep it up a bit longer. Go ahead with the float . . . and have fun. We'll take care of the Coopers."

We stood up. "I'm most grateful to you," Mr Menders said. "I thought we were hiring babysitters. I didn't realize you were detectives, too."

Outside, we found Georgio's truck parked next to the shed. He and Seth were carrying the plywood pieces we'd painted from the shed to the truck. Georgio flashed me a big grin. While we worked on the float I brought Georgio up-to-date on all that had happened during the storm.

It was a fun morning. I liked being with Georgio more than any guy I'd ever been with, and I loved building the float with him.

While we were working, we kept an eye open

for the "Coopers", but they didn't turn up.

After a while Mrs Menders asked Georgio and me to come with her to inspect the "Coopers'" rooms.

It didn't take us long to work out that the "Coopers" had moved out. Apart from the white gown, the drawers and cupboards were completely empty.

"They must have known we'd worked out what they were doing," I said. "And that we'd tell you about it."

"Which means you and the kids were in more danger than we realized," Georgio put in.

Mrs Menders shuddered.

I noticed a piece of spiral notebook paper on the desk. I handed it to Mrs Menders. "They left you a note," I said. She read it aloud.

> The house – and its ghosts – are yours.
>
> C.R.

"What will happen now?" I asked Mrs Menders.

"My husband is at the police station. I'll call there with this update. I expect the police will check the airports and see if they can stop the Coopers before they leave the country. But you shouldn't worry about it. We want you to have a fabulous time for the rest of your visit with us. Especially today."

At lunchtime we gathered on the verandah for a

make-your-own sandwich meal. Mr and Mrs Menders brought out a basket of bread and plates of meat, cheeses and vegetables. Georgio was invited to eat with us. We were all excited about the parade, but the Menders kids seemed to be the most excited of all.

When we'd sat down with our sandwiches, Lionel and Jason stood up and simultaneously took off their denim shirts, exposing T-shirts underneath that read *The Locals*.

"It's our team name," Jason said proudly. "Lionel talked the theatre into sponsoring us. All the guys on the team have shirts just like these. And we're marching in the parade. We want everyone to know who we are, because we're going to win the championship. Aren't we, Lionel?"

"You bet!" Lionel answered.

We cheered. Mr and Mrs Menders were smiling proudly at their sons.

After lunch Georgio went to the cottage to tidy up and dress for the parade. The rest of us went to our rooms to put on our costumes. I waited till I heard everyone else go downstairs before I left my room. Holding up the skirt of the floor-length gown so I wouldn't trip, I climbed the stairs to the third floor. Then, using the key Georgio had given me, I opened a door to another shorter flight of stairs. I climbed to the top, opened the door, and stepped out on to the widow's walk.

Claudia

My white satin gown shimmered in the bright sunlight.

The view of the sea from that height was so vast and beautiful it took my breath away. I remembered what the woman at the historical society had told Mary Anne about Mary Randolph. "I expect Mary Randolph grieved for her husband. Perhaps she even took to the widow's walk now and again." And when she did, I thought, she looked out at the sea that killed her husband and became his grave.

I looked towards the ground and saw the three-dimensional replica of the widow's walk that we'd mounted on the pickup truck. Everyone but me was gathered around it.

My friends looked outrageously elegant in their gowns. Kristy had on a red gown and Dawn was in the blue velvet one. Mary Anne wore the yellow gown with the smocking she had admired. The three of them would stand with me on the float.

Georgio was going to drive the float. He was wearing a Union Army uniform. And Andrew— in a sailor suit and carrying the antique toy boat he loved so much—would stand on the float with us babysitters. Jill, Martha and Karen were dressed in party dresses we'd found in an attic trunk. They would walk in front of the float carrying our banner.

I was surprised that no one had discovered me

standing on the widow's walk yet. I was about to shout, "Reginald!" to get their attention, when Jill looked up and spotted me.

"Look! It's *her*! The ghost!" Jill screamed.

"It's the Claudia ghost!" Dawn yelled.

Everyone was looking up at the widow's walk. I waved. They cheered and waved back.

And that's what being in the parade was like. We waved to the people along the route and they cheered and waved back to us. They loved our sign.

The Randolph Mansion wishes Reese a Happy Birthday!

After the parade, we went back to the mansion to change from our costumes into the outfits we'd wear for the carnival. Georgio was going to pick me up at seven.

I think I drove Dawn crazy while we were changing. Every time either one of us said something nice about Georgio, I'd add, "Do you think he's too old for me?" Dawn reminded me about her experience with an older guy called Travis. We agreed that Georgio was a lot nicer than Travis, who had thought he could make Dawn over into his idea of what a girlfriend should be. Still, Georgio was *older* than Travis.

During the carnival I successfully put the age

235

difference between me and Georgio out of my mind—at first. We rode the Ferris wheel; tossed rings at bottles; ate hot dogs, chips and candy-floss; threw darts; and rode the Ferris wheel again. As we were going up on the Ferris wheel for the second time, I really thought that maybe Georgio could be my boyfriend even though we live hundreds of miles apart. We could write letters, talk on the phone, and visit one another.

Our car stopped at the top. Georgio took my hand in his and said, "Claudia, I'd like you to come to homecoming weekend at my college. It's in October. There's a plane you can take to the airport near school—I've already checked. You don't have to answer now. But I want you to promise you'll think about it."

I promised. It wasn't a hard promise to keep. There was a lot to think about. How could I take a plane to Maine to be with a college student for a weekend when I was only thirteen years old? As well as the fact that my parents would never in a hundred million years let me, there was also the fact that Georgio thought I was sixteen!

I thought of Dawn's disastrous fling with Travis. And Stacey's doomed crush on a teacher. But, still, I did love being with Georgio. How could that be wrong?

When the Ferris wheel came to a stop, Mary Anne and Kristy were waiting for us. Kristy said she thought she'd seen Charles Randolph (alias

Claudia

Elton Cooper) near the merry-go-round. "And I think I saw Margaret Cooper," Mary Anne said in a frightened, trembling voice.

"Where did you see her?" I asked Mary Anne.

"Right here. Near the Ferris wheel."

So maybe they hadn't gone away. Maybe they were still in Reese and trying to catch us with our guard down. What if Mrs Cooper had been trying to interfere with the Ferris wheel to cause an accident? We spent the rest of the night looking for the Coopers at the carnival, and taking turns keeping an eye on the machines that ran the rides.

The mystery might not be over.

EPILOGUE

At breakfast on Sunday morning I found Mrs Menders and Mary Anne sitting at the table on the verandah. Mr and Mrs Menders had been out late the night before, so there hadn't been a chance to tell them about our possible sighting of Margaret Randolph. "Kristy and Dawn are making breakfast," Mary Anne told me. "You and I are on washing-up duty."

I looked over her shoulder and saw that she and Mrs Menders were making up a schedule of who would do what chores during our last few days in Reese. I was glad to see that they were including Karen and Andrew and the Menders children on the list.

"But this is still our holiday," Mrs Menders said. "Everyone should relax and have fun."

I hated to spoil her mood, but I had to tell her that we thought we'd seen Charles Randolph and his wife at the carnival.

Mrs Menders told me that I must have been mistaken. "Charles and Margaret Randolph are already back in Scotland," she said. "We've just had a phone call from the police saying the Randolphs left the country on a late flight from Boston."

"What are you going to do about them?" I asked.

"We may not do anything," Mrs Menders answered. "There aren't really any charges we can file. Unless they bother us again."

We had a great time during those last few days in Reese! With the adults around more of the time, and the Menders kids looking after one another, there were long stretches of time when we sitters didn't have even one kid to sit for. That left plenty of time for a thorough search of the attic for the treasure.

We didn't find a chest of gold coins and jewels. So we told the Menderses the story of what Mr Menders's uncle had said on his deathbed about the treasure in his attic.

"I think we have a big enough treasure in inheriting this wonderful property as our home," Mr Menders said. "Perhaps that's what Uncle Randolph meant. That the estate was his treasure and he wished he could take it with him in death."

I thought that was an interesting idea, but I wasn't sure I agreed. I had this nagging feeling there was a treasure we'd missed. I told myself that I shouldn't expect to solve the "Mystery of the Hidden Treasure", but be satisfied that we'd survived, and solved, the "Mystery of the Haunted House".

Dear Claudia:

You've been gone a day and I miss you already. I only spent ten days with you, so why does it feel like I've known you all my life?

The Menders kids are doing great. Everyone is happy that the "Coopers" are gone, including yours truly.

I'm counting on seeing you on homecoming weekend. We'll have a terrific time. There's a rock concert, a clambake on the beach, and of course a big dance. But October's so far away. Let's find a way to be together before that.

I have to go to work now, but will write a longer letter soon.

Here are some petals from our rose garden.

Love,
Georgio

Dear Georgio:

Thanks a lot for your great letter. I miss seeing you every day. I have something important to tell you. I'm thirteen years old. When you guessed I was sixteen I didn't tell you the truth. I'm sorry. I know you said you have friends all different ages. But six years is just too big a difference between us. For example, I can't go to homecoming weekend. My parents wouldn't let me. Besides, I'd feel out of place with all those college students.

Maybe when we're both older six years won't be such a big deal. Meanwhile, I hope I can be one of your friends who happens to be a girl.

Please write again soon.

Claudia

P.S.
I had a wonderful time with you in Reese, especially at the carnival.

Dear Becca,
I know I've been a lousy big sister to you lately. I feel awful about it. I'm really sorry. Will you forgive

me? I say it's time to do some serious Rollerblading. How about it?

Love,
Jessi

IOU 5 hours of Rollerblade Instruction

Dear Dawn, Kristy, Claudia, and Mary Anne,

Thank you for taking care of us. I like being a baby-sitter, too. Georgio found me a job as a mother's helper. I help Mrs. Johnson take care of Tammy. Tammy's four. ¼ sometimes. Martha helps me babysit for Tammy. I told Martha she could be a junior member of my baby-sitting club. Is that ok?

Your friend and fellow baby-sitter,
Jillian Menders

242

Dear Sitters:

Are you sitting down? You better be because I have big news. I got a small (but not too small) role in Our Town. Yes, I, Lionel, the pain-in-the-neck guy who complained that there was nothing to do in Reese. Now I'm complaining there's too much to do in Reese. I told my parents I have to go back to Boston for a rest.

Anyway, thanks for helping us city kids learn to like life in a small town.

Lionel

DEAR KRISTY:

YOU'RE A GOOD SOFTBALL PLAYER FOR A GIRL. THANK YOU FOR HELPING ME MAKE A TEAM. WE WON OUR FIRST GAME 10 TO 7. EVERYONE IN THE REC ROOM SAYS HI. IT STOPPED RAINING SO WE CAN PRACTICE NOW. GOTTA GO.

JASON

DEAR MARTHA:

HOW ARE YOU? HAVE YOU MADE ANY NEW FRIENDS LATELY? HOW IS THE SWIM TEAM? I HAD A GOOD TIME AT YOUR HOUSE. BEING IN THE PARADE WAS THE BEST. CAN YOU COME VISIT ME? I HAVE LOTS OF FRIENDS THAT YOU WOULD LOVE TO MEET. I WILL HAVE A BIG PARTY FOR YOU.

YOUR FRIEND,
KAREN

Dear Karen:

I have three new friends in Reese. If you were here we could have a party. My swim team is doing good. I win a lot of ribbons.

Your friend,
Martha

Dear Claudia :

How are you? We enjoyed your visits very much. I am writing to tell you what's happened to us since you left. At Georgio's suggestion we had tea at the mansion with Mr. and Mrs. Menders. As you may have heard, their caretaker couple left them quite suddenly. Mr. and Mrs. Menders asked us if we would like to come out of retirement and work part time for them. The next day Georgio helped us move back into our little house by the pond. I am writing this note in my garden.

Our warm regards to you and the other members of your club. I learned all about it from Jill while we were baking.

Sincerely,
Bertha Tiono

244

~~DOROTHY~~

DEAR MR. AND MRS. MENDERS:
I HAD A GOOD TIME AT
YOUR HOUSE. YOUR HOUSE
IS BIG. THANK YOU FOR GIVING
ME THE BOAT. KRISTY AND ME
CLEANED IT. THERE WAS
WRITING ON THE SIDE. IT
SAID, "TREASURE." KRISTY
SAID TO TELL YOU, " THE
BOAT WAS THE TREASURE IN
THE ATTIC."
                    ANDREW

P.S.
KRISTY HELPED ME WRITE
THIS LETTER. SHE SAYS, HI!

When our Reese holiday was over, I still had to write my summer essay for Mrs Hall. I reread our Reese notebook and thought about how to organize all that had happened to us in Reese. In those ten days I had acquired an awful lot to write about.

I decided to start at the beginning, with our first night in the Randolph mansion, and then to let the story unfold. I was nervous before I started writing, but once I began it was easier than I had thought it would be. I typed the second draft of my paper on Janine's computer and used the spellcheck. Then I gave my paper a title—THE MYSTERY OF THE HAUNTED HOUSE— included my drawings of the mansion, and handed it in.

Guess what? I got an A!

The Babysitters Club

Need a babysitter? Then call the Babysitters Club. Kristy Thomas and her friends are all experienced sitters. They can tackle any job from rampaging toddlers to a pandemonium of pets. To find out all about them, read on!

1. Kristy's Great Idea
2. Claudia and the Phantom Phone Calls
3. The Truth About Stacey
4. Mary Anne Saves The Day
5. Dawn and the Impossible Three
6. Kristy's Big Day
7. Claudia and Mean Janine
8. Boy-Crazy Stacey
9. The Ghost At Dawn's House
10. Logan Likes Mary Anne!
11. Kristy and the Snobs
12. Claudia and the New Girl
13. Goodbye Stacey, Goodbye
14. Hello, Mallory
15. Little Miss Stoneybrook ... and Dawn
16. Jessi's Secret Language
17. Mary Anne's Bad-Luck Mystery
18. Stacey's Mistake
19. Claudia and the Bad Joke
20. Kristy and the Walking Disaster
21. Mallory and the Trouble With Twins
22. Jessi Ramsey, Pet-Sitter
23. Dawn On The Coast
24. Kristy and the Mother's Day Surprise
25. Mary Anne and the Search For Tigger
26. Claudia and the Sad Goodbye
27. Jessi and the Superbrat
28. Welcome Back, Stacey!
29. Mallory and the Mystery Diary
30. Mary Anne and the Great Romance
31. Dawn's Wicked Stepsister

32. Kristy and the Secret Of Susan
33. Claudia and the Great Search
34. Mary Anne and Too Many Boys
35. Stacey and the Mystery Of Stoneybrook
36. Jessi's Babysitter
37. Dawn and the Older Boy
38. Kristy's Mystery Admirer
39. Poor Mallory!
40. Claudia and the Middle School Mystery
41. Mary Anne Vs. Logan
42. Jessi and the Dance School Phantom
43. Stacey's Emergency
44. Dawn and the Big Sleepover
45. Kristy and the Baby Parade
46. Mary Anne Misses Logan
47. Mallory On Strike
48. Jessi's Wish
49. Claudia and the Genius Of Elm Street
50. Dawn's Big Date
51. Stacey's Ex-Best Friend
52. Mary Anne and Too Many Babies
53. Kristy For President
54. Mallory and the Dream Horse
55. Jessi's Gold Medal
56. Keep Out, Claudia!
57. Dawn Saves The Planet
58. Stacey's Choice
59. Mallory Hates Boys (and Gym)
60. Mary Anne's Makeover
61. Jessi and the Awful Secret
62. Kristy and the Worst Kid Ever
63. Claudia's Freind Friend
64. Dawn's Family Feud
65. Stacey's Big Crush
66. Maid Mary Anne
67. Dawn's Big Move
68. Jessi and the Bad Babysitter
69. Get Well Soon, Mallory!
70. Stacey and the Cheerleaders
71. Claudia and the Perfect Boy
72. Dawn and the We Love Kids Club
73. Mary Anne and Miss Priss
74. Kristy and the Copycat
75. Jessi's Horrible Prank
76. Stacey's Lie

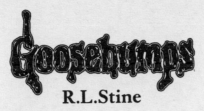

R.L. Stine

Reader beware, you're in for a scare!
These terrifying tales will send shivers up your spine:

1 Welcome to Dead House
2 Say Cheese and Die!
3 Stay out of the Basement
4 The Curse of the Mummy's Tomb
5 Monster Blood
6 Let's Get Invisible
7 Night of the Living Dummy
8 The Girl Who Cried Monster
9 Welcome to Camp Nightmare
10 The Ghost Next Door
11 The Haunted Mask
12 Piano Lessons Can Be Murder
13 Be Careful What You Wish For
14 The Werewolf of Fever Swamp
15 You Can't Scare Me
16 One Day at Horrorland
17 Why I'm Afraid of Bees
18 Monster Blood II
19 Deep Trouble
20 Go Eat Worms
21 Return of the Mummy
22 The Scarecrow Walks at Midnight
23 Attack of the Mutant
24 My Hairiest Adventure
25 A Night in Terror Tower
26 The Cuckoo Clock of Doom
27 Monster Blood III
28 Ghost Beach
29 Phantom of the Auditorium
30 It Came From Beneath the Sink!
31 Night of the Living Dummy II
32 The Barking Ghost
33 The Horror at Camp Jellyjam